THE TRAILBLAZER

BOSTON HAWKS HOCKEY
BOOK 7

GINA AZZI

THREE CITIES PUBLISHING LLC

PROLOGUE
VIVI

"A marriage stipulation?"

"That's right," Granddaddy's lawyer, Mr. Rhett, says. His gaze is not without compassion, and I latch onto that, trying to understand why Granddaddy would make my stake in the Harrison Foundation contingent upon *marriage*.

Tears fill my eyes and I avert my gaze, clearing my throat. Granddaddy was cremated yesterday morning and since his passing, nothing has felt right. Nothing has made a lick of sense. And now…this. My leadership in the Harrison Foundation, in my life's purpose, is conditional on my marrying. How could Granddaddy put me in this position? How could the man who raised me, the man I loved with every fiber of my being, allow my future to depend on a man? On my *submission* to a man?

The thoughts tumble in my mind, but I can't process them. It doesn't make sense. Granddaddy was hardly traditional and yet…

"When did he add this condition?" I ask.

Mr. Rhett glances down at the last will and testament of Beau Harrison, clutched in his hand. "Mr. Harrison amended his will two weeks ago."

Two weeks! What happened two weeks ago to necessitate this ridiculous change?

"And if Vivi doesn't marry...?" my cousin Alfred cuts in.

I roll my eyes. Isn't it enough that Alfred received one hundred percent of the shares in Harrison Lumber, Granddaddy's bread and butter? Now, he's going to have decision-making power in the Harrison Foundation too? My business-savvy cousin isn't a bad guy, he just has a completely different outlook than me. His worldview is more profit driven, with an absolute fixation on the bottom line.

As equal partners in running the foundation, Alfred and I will always be at an impasse. He'll want to cut programs to focus on one or two initiatives and tighten our spending, while I want to expand our reach. If we're partners, the relationships, the network, everything I've spent the past seven years building will falter.

What will become of the philanthropic causes Granddaddy fostered and I care so much about? Breast cancer awareness. Literacy campaigns. Lupus research. The food shelters the Harrison Foundation funds throughout the country. The youth outreach programs.

Alfred's approach isn't in line with the mission of the foundation. His outlook doesn't match the spirit of the work, the legacy I thought Granddaddy trusted me to continue.

A new thought enters my mind, making me nauseous. Did Granddaddy think I can't handle it? That I can't run the foundation on my own? Then, why did he keep giving me more responsibilities? Were they a test, instead of a reward? Oh God, did he find me lacking?

The Harrison Foundation has been my salvation. I started working there right out of high school, forgoing college, to expand its philanthropic outreach. I've worked on programs throughout the country, increasing our reach, the scope of our work, and the thousands of people who benefit from our programs. And now, I learn that...Granddaddy wasn't pleased with my performance? Or confident enough that I could pick up the torch he laid down and continue the work?

Absentmindedly, I lift my hand, wrapping it around the base of my throat. The realization hurts even more than not having complete control over the direction of the foundation. The thought that Granddaddy wasn't proud of me cuts nearly as deep as his death. And now, he's not even here for me to ask why? Why keep me connected to the foundation in a reduced capacity? Why not cut me lose completely? Why state that I must marry before my twenty-fifth birthday to lead the foundation on my own? And, why oh why, put me in this compromising position with Alfred?

"We can make this work, Genevieve." My cousin grins. "I promise not to shut down all of the programs. Just the ones bleeding us dry." He sighs, plucking at his lip. At my expression, his grin falls. "You can still keep the women's programs."

My nausea intensifies, churning dangerously in my stomach.

"Hush, Alfred." Aunt Marge, Alfred's mother, places her hand on her son's shoulder. Her eyes are also sympathetic, and I hate that everyone is regarding me with pity. Granddaddy's will was a shock, not just to me, but to my small family. For years, he's been grooming Alfred to take over his business and me to run the future of his charity work.

"Who will you marry?" Aunt Marge asks. "Your birthday is next week."

I cut her a look, the blood draining from my face.

Who the hell will I marry? I don't have a boyfriend or a guy I'm dating. Hell, except for Henry, I don't even have friends.

Who is going to marry me in one week? Who would even want that role?

I stand shakily, my knees knocking together. Placing a hand on my stomach, I croak, "Excuse me." Then, I flee from

Granddaddy's office, rush down the hall, and make it just in time to empty the contents of my stomach into the toilet.

For a woman who has spent the past seven years mostly on my own, this feels like a new low. Achingly acute loneliness cuts through me as I realize I have no one I can count on.

As usual, there's only myself.

CHAPTER 1
DECLAN

The arena pulses with energy, an infectious excitement and enthusiasm for tonight's game that carries into the locker room.

It washes over me, demanding that I mentally lock in. It hypes me up, reminding me how fortunate I am. How many people turn their childhood dream into reality? How many little kids with a pair of skates and a hockey stick dream of playing in the NHL?

It's my first season starting for the Boston Hawks and each time I take the ice, gratitude for my stubbornness, persistence, and the luck of the Irish, mainly in the form of Beau Harrison, the man who paved my way for a hockey career, rolls through me. I take a deep breath and try to calm my nerves. I toss up a prayer and move to close my locker door when my phone buzzes with an incoming call.

As soon as Da's name flashes across the screen, a ball of dread forms in the pit of my stomach. Something's happened. There's no way Da would call right before a game, a game he's most likely tuning into, unless something is wrong.

"Da, what's wrong?" I answer immediately.

He sighs. "I'm sorry, Declan. Mr. Harrison passed."

His words slam into me with the strength of a slap shot: hard, quick, and devastating. I gesture to a guy on my team that I'm stepping out to talk to Da. Once in the hallway, I sink down onto a bench, gripping the phone until my knuckles pop.

"When?" I whisper, my tone raw with emotion.

"Four days ago."

"Four days? When's the funeral?" A note of panic laces my tone. Did I miss it? Miss saying goodbye to the man who shaped my future?

"The family had a small, private ceremony. He was cremated. I'm sorry, son. I know how much he meant to you." Da sighs, "There aren't many men like Beau left in the world."

How's Vivi? I'm desperate to ask but years of silence between me and the girl who once owned my heart causes me to hold my tongue. Instead, I work a swallow, guilt expanding through my chest. "I just spoke to him two, maybe three weeks ago. He asked me to send some signed hockey gear for one of the youth camps his foundation runs. He was so...proud."

"He was always proud of you," Da agrees. Da worked as the head grounds caretaker on Beau Harrison's estate my entire childhood. It wasn't until I started university that Da moved back to his native Ireland. At that point, Mr. Harrison's granddaughter Vivi and I had broken up and without Da or Vivi to visit in Tennessee, Mr. Harrison became my only point of contact in the place that raised me. And now, he's gone... "How did he die?"

"A heart attack. He's been having trouble for quite some time. He just kept it quiet. I only heard occasional updates from Mrs. Stevens," Da explains, referencing another employee of Mr. Harrison's. "Genevieve's taking it hard."

Vivi. My heart twists thinking of her. How is she handling the news? Is she alone, walking the halls of the mansion she was raised in? Or maybe in a downtown bar, drinking to her granddaddy's legacy with a group of friends. I frown, realizing I know nothing about her life now. I know nothing about her.

But the last time I spoke to Mr. Harrison… "He asked me to look out for her. When I spoke to him, he asked me, and I laughed it off. He knew…" I trail off again, trying to make sense of the news. "I haven't spoken to Vivi in seven years." But I've never stopped thinking of Genevieve Rae, my Vivi. She was the one that got away, the one I never got over. Even though I clung to my relationship with her granddaddy all these years, we never spoke of Vivi. Not until that last conversation…

"Well, if you don't get to Nashville by tomorrow, you won't be able to honor that request." Da's brogue is thicker, filled with emotion and the pain of losing his old friend.

"What are you talking about?" I demand.

"She's getting married."

Those three words stop me short. They pull something in my chest, something I locked away years ago, until it unravels, unravelling me.

"To whom?" I whisper, a new type of fear skating up my arms. There's no way Vivi wouldn't postpone her wedding in the wake of her granddaddy's death. Mr. Harrison was more like a father to Vivi anyway. Her mom died in childbirth and her dad is a career military officer, usually deployed. Vivi wouldn't celebrate anything, much less a wedding, five goddamn days after Mr. Harrison's passing. Something is off; it doesn't *feel* right. "This doesn't make any sense."

"Henry Stevens," Da offers, naming Mrs. Stevens' son, one of my childhood buddies. Henry, Vivi, and I grew up together on the Harrison Estate.

Memories of long forgotten days roll through my mind with sharp precision. Henry, Genevieve, and me swinging from a rope into the creek, climbing trees, racing each other to the top, bike riding around town, and eating ice cream cones on Saturday afternoons. While Vivi and Henry were close, we always knew, all three of us, that Vivi and I were forever. That our connection outpaced any childhood friendship or adolescent puppy love.

At least, I thought we did. Until Vivi and I broke up the summer before college, I went to Ireland with Da, and she stopped returning my calls. Instead of the friendship we promised each other, Vivi stomped all over my heart, and we moved down two different paths with two very different endings.

Genevieve Rae is marrying Henry Stevens.

The words don't compute in my brain because they're all fucking wrong. She can't marry him. She can't marry…

But can't she? An old memory, one I worked hard to forget, flairs to life in my mind. The one time I returned to Tennessee after leaving for the University of Minnesota. It was my sophomore year of college and I had to see her; I had to know why she cut me off the way she did. When I hugged her goodbye before my trip, we swore we'd still talk, that we'd be in each other's lives no matter what. I tried. Why didn't she?

When I saw her with Henry, I knew. They were laughing, messing around with boxing gloves behind the small house Henry's family occupied. He was training her but his hands, they touched her with familiarity, with confidence. The blustering friend of my childhood had grown into a man who knew my girl better than I did.

Unable to stomach it, I left. I haven't seen her since.

The cheers from the arena reverberate down the hallway, capturing my attention again.

"Da, I appreciate you calling but I'm about to skate out on—"

"Hockey isn't everything, son." Da's voice holds an edge, something I don't fully understand.

"We broke up," I remind him. "We haven't talked in years."

"Have you not thought of her in that long too?"

I swear, because Da knows damn well that not a day passes without my thinking of Genevieve. About the promises we made and the future we dreamed up. About the friendship we swore meant everything, no matter where we went to college, no matter what happened afterwards.

But then I left for Minnesota and she...fell in love with Henry fucking Stevens. I saw it with my own eyes the following year.

"It's not too late," Da murmurs. "You've still got time, son."

"Time for what?" I scoff, frustrated and angry and so fucking gutted by the news Da shared. Mr. Harrison is dead. Vivi's getting married. The arena is waiting. My head spins, my emotions pulled in too many conflicting directions.

"To get your girl."

"Right," I say sarcastically. "I gotta go, Da." I hang up.

But I don't stand from the bench. Instead, I fist my phone and feel the gut-wrenching sadness of Mr. Harrison's loss mix with the terrifying realization that I can't lose Vivi. Not forever, not without knowing what went wrong, not without...telling her that I never truly moved on.

Before I can overthink it, I pull off my jersey and re-enter the silent locker room. I change into sweats. I rush down the hallway of The Meadows, away from the arena, toward the parking lot and my waiting SUV. I blow off a NHL hockey game as a defenseman for the Boston Hawks, the career opportunity of a lifetime, to drive seventeen hours to break up a wedding. But not any wedding. Vivi's.

I LOST MY FUCKING MIND.

It's the only thing that makes sense as the high of adrenaline, the wave of fear, I've been riding for nearly seventeen hours on my drive home to Tennessee morphs into fatigue.

I take the turn toward my tiny hometown, on the outskirts of Nashville. My parents moved here when I was a kid, my father's family unhappy that he fell for an American instead of an Irishwoman. It was hypocritical bullshit if you ask me since my father's mother married a German. But we don't talk about my grandfather, the guy who hit it and quit it, leaving nothing behind but his last name and a dark stain on my family's reputation in a small, Irish village.

After mom passed when I was five, Da stayed in Tennessee, happily employed by Mr. Harrison. It wasn't until I accepted a hockey scholarship to the University of Minnesota that Da agreed to move back to his homeland.

While my whole family now resides in Ireland, the one I made as a child in Tennessee still claims a piece of my soul. Genevieve Rae still holds a piece of my heart.

Which is why, after seventeen long hours, I enter the small town we both call home, and scan every passerby for her wild, blonde waves and bright, sky blue eyes.

Driving down Main Street, my life in Boston falls away. Instead, I see a million memories from before Boston and the NHL, from before hockey. I see Vivi eating strawberry ice cream cones with chocolate sprinkles. Mrs. Grant in her green apron, waving us past her shop on our bicycles, after stuffing our pockets with candy. I see the old public library where Vivi taught me how to read and the corner store where I bought her a bracelet for her twelfth birthday. That was the first time she kissed me, and I don't know if I ever truly came up for oxygen since. Because when my lips touched hers, everything I thought I knew disappeared and everything I thought I wanted changed.

I wanted her.

Shaking my head, I turn off Main Street toward a bed-and-breakfast Da told me Mrs. Cleary still runs in the heart of the historic district. I park my SUV and grab the small bag I keep in the back for emergencies—usually of the hockey variety—but right now, I'm glad it's stocked with two changes of clothes, clean underwear, and a toothbrush. It also holds a couple hundred-dollar bills and my passport, which is a relief, since I left my wallet in my locker at The Meadows. Shouldering my bag, I make my way inside.

Mrs. Cleary turns and smiles when the bell alerts her to my arrival but when she spots me her mouth drops open and tears spring to the corners of her eyes.

"Declan Yaeger, my word, is that really you?" she asks, her hands gripping the skirt of her dress.

I smile, knowing the moment my dimple pops because Mrs. Cleary's expression softens. "It's me, Mrs. C."

"Oh, welcome home," she sighs, hurrying around the counter and wrapping me up in a big hug that feels the same as it did when I was nine and flipped over the handlebars of my bike out front.

I breathe in the cinnamon and sugar that clings to her, years of making scones before the rest of town is awake, and feel a strange sensation move through my chest. The world suddenly shifts, straightens, and a wave of homesickness, a longing for what was, crashes over me.

Mrs. Cleary grips my shoulders and pulls back, offering a hopeful smile. "You're here for her, aren't you?"

I nod, my brow furrowing. "How'd you know?"

She laughs lightly. "Genevieve has that effect."

I smile. She sure does.

"Besides, we haven't seen you here in years."

Her words cause guilt to swell inside but I bite the corner of my mouth and nod in acknowledgement. There's no way I'm going to admit that the one time I did come home, my heart splintered all over again. After that, it never made sense. Why would I come back here if I wasn't coming home to Genevieve?

But right now, staring at Mrs. Cleary, noting the gray strands running through her hair, the wrinkles bracketing her mouth, I feel ashamed for staying away so long.

"We're all really proud of you, Declan," she says, making me feel worse.

"Thank you," I say quietly, undeserving of her praise. I never would have made it as far as I did without the support of Mr. Harrison. His commitment to me, to hockey, created my future. Him and Vivi and Da. This town. "Does she love him?" I dip my head, unsure if I want the answer.

She must, right? Genevieve Rae wouldn't marry for anything less than love. But how could anything be greater than what we once had?

Mrs. Cleary grips my hand and squeezes until I meet her eyes. "He's a good man."

I nod again, the movement jerky. Henry Stevens is a decent, caring guy. He'll make a good husband, a good father.

"They been together long?" I can't help myself from being a goddamn gossip when I want every morsel of information pertaining to Vivi. Everything and anything I missed over the past seven years, even though I have no right to it, to her, anymore.

Mrs. Cleary tips her head, studying me. "You don't know, do you?"

"Know what?" My voice is hushed, as if the fear of knowing holds it back. Does Vivi hate me? Is she pregnant? Is she in trouble? My throat burns as the thoughts tumble through my mind.

"Henry and Genevieve…" Mrs. Cleary trails off, collecting her thoughts and words, and an irrational surge of dislike rises toward my old friend.

But why shouldn't Henry have Vivi? He stuck around all

these years. He stayed while I...left. Left and never really looked back.

"Well, they're doing right by their families, whatever that means," she says finally, leaving me with more questions. "Come." Mrs. Cleary taps my arm before turning back to the front desk. "Let's get you checked in and showered. Ceremony's at three." She looks up at me. "You have two hours, Declan. Use them."

I nod, following her. Now that I'm here, that strange adrenaline mixed with fear is back, wiping out my fatigue and filling me up with a restlessness that borders on panic.

I need to see Vivi. I need to talk to Henry. I need to mourn Mr. Harrison. I need to know when the hell everything changed so much, and why I didn't realize it until now.

SOME OF MY questions are answered only an hour later as I stand to the side of the church, pacing back and forth, my mind racing. All the emotions of coming home are warring for space in my mind, but I shut them down, focused on Genevieve.

After calling Da to let him know I arrived in Nashville, I quietly enter the church, only to catch my first glimpse of her. And it nearly breaks me.

Genevieve Rae is a vision. She's always been beautiful but now, as a woman, she's stunning. Her golden hair is curled and pulled away from her face, showing off her cheekbones and the delicate slope of her neck. Her lips are a perfect Cupid's bow, begging to be kissed. Her eyes are just as blue as I remember.

But that's where the similarities end. Because the fun-loving, spunky, loud, and giggly girl from my past is now an intense, unreadable force of a woman.

Her voice is even as she stands by the altar, exchanging words with the priest, Father Ward. But she wrings her hands, and I can tell she's nervous, just doing her best to hide it.

Father Ward nods and moves out of the church through a side door. Vivi's shoulders drop a fraction but then the door opens again, and I watch as she straightens, her body tense.

She turns slowly and as she does, she relaxes and a smile that could light up New York City washes over her face. My hands curl into fists as Henry Stevens strides down the aisle. What the hell is he doing here? Isn't it bad luck to see the bride before the wedding?

But nothing about this wedding seems traditional. The timing, the reaction of Mrs. Cleary when she saw me, the bride and the groom meeting before the ceremony, it all indicates a sense of urgency I don't understand.

Henry's expression is serious and Vivi's smile morphs into a look of concern. She holds out her hands as he reaches her. He takes them, pulling her forward to wrap her in a big hug. He holds her for a long moment, both of their eyes closed. They look sad, almost hopeless. Absolutely nothing like a couple about to embark on their happily-ever-after.

Vivi pulls away first but keeps her hands tucked in Henry's. "You can't go through with it, can you?"

"You look beautiful, Viv." Henry kisses both of her cheeks.

I frown, straining to hear their words without giving away my presence. What the hell is going on?

"Henry," Vivi says.

"I can't go through with it," he murmurs, his eyes closing, as if in pain. "I can't live the lie."

"I understand," Vivi states without a trace of anger. "I'm so sorry I ever asked you to."

"No." Henry shakes his head. "I'd do anything for you,

Viv. I just, I *can't* do this. I can't keep hiding like this. I need to tell him."

"It's okay." Vivi shrugs and offers him a lopsided grin.

"It's not," Henry argues with her. He reaches up to stop a tear that falls from her eye and my body coils in anticipation.

Why is she crying? Why is he jilting her? What the hell is he talking about, a lie?

Henry swears and shakes his head. "I hate myself for standing by and watching you lose everything."

"Not everything." She gives him a sad smile.

He shakes his head, his jaw clenched.

"I'll be okay, Henry."

Henry clucks, his expression filled with admiration for Vivi. "Only you, Viv. Only you manage to land on your feet. It's not fair that you're always taking care of everyone, with no one looking out for you. I hate that I'm—"

"Stop," Vivi cuts him off and shakes her head. She clings to his wrist, holding on to him like a lifeline.

I work a swallow, anger rushing through me. Why is she forgiving him so easily for jilting her? Why doesn't she seem angry at all? I'm angry *for* her. And what the hell does Henry mean, no one is looking out for Vivi? Isn't that *his* job, as her fiancé?

"Viv…" Henry cups her cheek, his other hand hooking around her hip to draw her closer. She stumbles forward and I let out a low growl. "You and I both know this is bigger than us. You can't lose the foundation. If Alfred and you…" He trails off and sighs. "So much of the good you're doing will suffer."

Vivi shakes her head, her smile soft, her eyes sad. "But I can't lose you, Henry. I can figure out the foundation stuff and deal with Alfred, but not at the expense of us."

My confusion ratchets up several more notches. Isn't she losing him now? If he leaves her here, in church, on their wedding day, what the hell will be salvageable of their relationship? What am I missing?

Henry clears his throat. "If we do this…"

"Henry, no." Vivi shakes her head. Her eyes close and I watch her shoulders sag. Is she disappointed? Relieved?

Whatever she is, it sure as fuck isn't the fury that races through my body, turning my blood hot. Henry's gonna leave her at the altar? And tell her this on their goddamn wedding day while standing in church?

"Viv…" Henry's thumb swipes along her cheekbone. "You need to get married, babe, and if not me, then who?"

Hurt blazes over Vivi's face, her expression crumpling as Henry's words ring true. It's the dejected acceptance in her eyes that breaks me free of the spell holding my tongue.

I step forward and without thinking about what the hell I'm agreeing to, I announce, "Me."

CHAPTER 2
VIVI

"M e." Declan Yaeger steps out from behind a column in church like a memory from my past.

My breath catches in my throat and an overwhelming sense of déjà vu rocks through me, causing me to stumble back. For a moment, I see him the way I remember him. As a high school hockey player on the cusp of manhood. The guy who picked me up for my senior prom, moving between the columns in front of Granddaddy's house, a corsage in his hand. My fingertips press against my lips and an unattractive sound splits the air, half laugh, half sob.

Henry's hold on me tightens, keeping me upright. Declan's expression twists and then, he's beside me. My world spins so hard, I wonder if it will break into a million pieces, like a kaleidoscope. Nothing makes sense right now. *Nothing.*

Henry, my fiancé, my oldest and truest friend, can't marry me without betraying himself. I never should have asked him to and standing here now, my guilt for putting him in this position crashes down on me.

His honesty shames me. The summer Declan left and my

life changed forever, Henry told me, *"I'll always be here for you, Viv. Whatever you need. I've got you."*

Surely he didn't mean marriage. And I was just desperate enough to take him up on the offer to marry me when...I should have known better.

I drop my hold on Henry. Instead, my hand rises to my throat and rests there, the beating of my heart faster than a hummingbird's wings. I feel the blood drain from my face as shame I've never known hollows me from the inside out. I nearly ruined my best friend's life for...my career.

But it's not *just* my career. It's Granddaddy's legacy, it's my grandmother's dream, it's all the good they managed to leave behind when they departed this world. And they entrusted it, at least half of it, to me.

Ooh, the words of Granddaddy's will, the shock of it all, still clings to the edges of my mind. When Mr. Rhett read the marriage stipulation, Aunt Marge, Alfred, and I all gasped. Now, five days later, I'm standing in a church, *trying* to marry. If my current position wasn't so desperate, I'd laugh at the absurdity of it all.

On top of my predicament, I feel awful that I'd nearly trapped Henry into a loveless marriage when he can have a crack at the real thing. At the thing I once shared with Declan.

Declan. I turn my head and he shifts closer, until he's standing before me. His cologne washes over me like a memory and oh, God, how I've missed him. His presence conjures up a thousand feelings I thought I laid to rest. I shiver and Declan's hand settles on my hip, its weight both a thrill and a warning.

I should be confused. Or hurt. Or anything except relieved. But...

"What are you doing here?" I whisper.

"Vivi." My name falling from his mouth causes tears to well in my eyes.

"Why now? Today?" I ask. It's been years and yet, here he is, offering *marriage*. On my wedding day.

Declan's gray eyes, so familiar and yet foreign, pierce mine, and my confusion grows, threatening to pull me under like quicksand. How did he know I was getting married today? Why does he care?

"What are you doing here, man?" Henry repeats my question.

"What the hell are you doing agreeing to marry her if you're not all in?" Declan retorts, his tone hard. But his voice, it's all man now, raspy and rough and…angry.

I like that he's angry on my behalf because that means a part of him must still care about me, right? Even though we broke up years ago, that summer is still fresh in my mind. The ease with which Declan galivanted off to Ireland, charmed women in pubs across Dublin, and never looked back ached as I dealt with the aftermath of our decisions on my own.

Still, I can't deny the strange comfort I feel that he's here. Just when things were starting to spiral, just when I was about to embark on a new low by marrying my best friend, a man not in love with me, Declan showed up. He showed up for me and that realization is strangely comforting. It's a balm to an old hurt, a concern for my well-being that didn't materialize when I miscarried our baby all those years ago. Even though he still doesn't know, even though my silence then was unfair to him, I couldn't help but feel resentful that while I wallowed through the aftermath completely alone, he was tossing back pints of Guinness.

But now, he's *here*.

I swallow and shake my head to clear my thoughts. I need to focus on the matter at hand, my ridiculous wedding day. I move forward, tripping over my dress. Declan wraps his arm around my waist and steadies me as I collide with the hard muscle of his chest. His warmth seeps into my skin, a reminder that this time, right now, I'm *not* alone. That maybe, I can still pull this off.

I clasp Declan's shoulders to keep myself upright and roll my lips together, my head spinning, as the overwhelming sensation of being wrapped in his arms spreads through my limbs.

Even in heels, I'm eye level with the base of his throat, tanned and smooth and working a concerned swallow. I feel his stare on the top of my head, worried and confused, and hate how much his presence still affects me. But everything about Declan Yaeger always made me feel something, made me feel too much, and this moment is no different.

I'm about to be left at the altar and the man who broke my heart is my only glimpse of hope, but that tiny glimmer of possibility keeps me rooted in place. Right now, to safeguard Granddaddy's legacy and my own purpose, I'll marry the man who spoiled every relationship that came after him just by existing. Just by being the irritating unit of measurement no other guy stacked up against.

I study him slowly, taking my time to look up from his strong shoulders. The hardness of his jaw, covered in a delicious scruff that I've never seen him sport before. At least, not in person. His mouth is clamped closed, a troubled slash I remember as a charming smile. Sculpted cheekbones, gray eyes that rival a thunderstorm, and sweet curls that used to be a source of ridicule but now soften Declan's strong features. His hair is brown with a reddish tint that speaks to his Irish roots. God, he's beautiful. Sexy.

And so unworthy of my foolish thoughts. I'm not sixteen and in love anymore. I'm a grown woman trying to safeguard the legacy my grandparents left behind.

I close my eyes to collect myself. When I open them, Declan's scowl has eased. Both of his hands are now resting on my hips, and my fingers are twisting the material of his shirt.

"You in trouble, Vivi?" Declan's eyebrows pull together, a line forming between them.

It catches me off guard, the realization that seven years have passed since I've seen him and yet…his hold on me feels as natural as ever.

"Viv, look at me," Henry commands.

I turn my head and stare at my best friend.

"You're not seriously considering this," Henry scoffs when he correctly reads my expression. Because I am seriously considering this. Marrying Declan makes sense on a strange level. We have a shared history, a shared respect. Fine, things didn't end on great terms but before we were lovers, we were the best of friends. I know I can trust him. I know he'd never hurt me or use my work, the foundation, against me.

And, maybe the most important part, I know that there's no future for us. Just like I knew there was no future for Henry and me. This marriage is an arrangement on paper only and allows me to pour all of my attention and dedication into the foundation.

I'm not offering up my heart. With the hurt between us, the loss of a baby, there's no chance I'll do something dumb like fall back in love with him. But why is he offering to marry me?

"Why would you offer to *marry* me?" I ask. "You don't even know me anymore. That summer, when I—"

Henry interrupts, "Why the hell are you showing up now? Where the fuck have you been the past seven years?"

The energy in the church shifts, the walls seeming to close in on us. Suddenly, it feels like I'm teetering on a tightrope, with my arms pulled in two different directions. Forward, toward the future, and backward, stuck in the past.

Declan moves and seems to grow three inches as his anger expands, something I can't decipher blazing from the depths of his eyes. He widens his stance and folds his arms across his chest. At the loss of his touch, my body turns cold and a flare of awareness, of *longing*, flickers to life in the pit of my stomach.

I've never seen this side of Declan before, and I'm captivated. He isn't the teenage boy I gave all my firsts to. No, he's all man and I feel sad that I missed out on witnessing that transition.

"I don't owe you anything," Declan spits before his eyes find mine again. "And I owe you a hell of a lot more than what you got." His eyes burn, nearly midnight, as he holds my gaze.

It almost sounds like an apology and a wave of emotion breaks free at the severity of his expression. I open my mouth but before I can speak, he cuts me off.

"What are you doing, Vivi?"

I frown.

"I may not know your favorite cocktail or who you read in college—"

"She didn't go to college," Henry interjects.

Surprise registers in Declan's eyes but his hand finds mine and tightens. "But I know you. There's no chance in hell you'd marry for anything less than love if you weren't in trouble. Tell me."

Tell me. Another command. If a different guy said it, even Henry, I'd have my hackles up. But with Declan, my lips part and the truth tumbles out.

"Granddaddy died. Last week."

"I know, baby. And I'm so fucking sorry." Declan's expression softens, sympathy sweeping through his eyes.

"I've been working for his foundation since I graduated high school. The past few years, I've taken on a leadership role. We're doing a lot of good work. Important work that benefits people—women and children—all over the country."

Pride flares in Declan's eyes and I like seeing it there. The foundation has been my sole priority, the thing that's kept me moving forward and I like that he's proud of it. Especially since I'm so unbelievably proud of him. Even though we parted on less than stellar terms, even though we both broke promises and let each other down, I've never stopped rooting for him. "At the reading of Granddaddy's will, my cousin Alfred was named the majority shareholder and CEO of the lumber business. While I thought I'd be running the foundation…" I trail off, heat spreading over my cheeks. I don't want to sound ungrateful for all that Granddaddy has left me, especially after he raised me when Mom passed and Dad was deployed, but… "there's a marriage stipulation."

"Huh?" Declan looks as confused as I felt at the reading.

"If I marry, by the time I'm twenty-five," I start.

"Which is in three days," Declan points out.

I nod. "Then, I lead the Harrison Foundation. I'll manage the programs and funds, the selection of board members, all the big decisions."

"Everything," Henry reiterates, and Declan's eyes widen.

"If not, Alfred and I will become partners, working together as equals, to ensure the foundation's future. And it's not about the title or status," I rush to explain.

"Never was with you, Vivi," Declan agrees.

"It's just that Alfred has a different vision than I do. He's very profit driven, which I can respect in business. But the foundation isn't like the lumber company. At its core is philanthropy. We don't make decisions in the name of profit, but in the spirit of doing meaningful work, at creating change, at offering options and resources. With the leadership being split, Alfred and I will never agree. I'm worried that so much of the progress the foundation has created will stop. That all the work I did won't have the impact I hoped."

Declan watches me for a long moment, his eyes searching. He turns to Henry suddenly, "And you were going to marry her to what, keep the legacy of the foundation intact?"

Henry smirks. "Among other things."

Declan frowns before shaking his head. "Vivi, your heart's

too damn big." His voice is raspy, filled with affection I didn't expect. "I don't know about the intricacies of Mr. Harrison's will or why he would make a marriage stipulation. I'm sure he had his reasons. But if you're marrying anyone today, it'll be me."

"Why?" I whisper, desperate to understand the motivation behind his offer. A small seed of hope sprouts and I try to tamp it down before it grows a flower.

Regret flickers in his irises, coloring them charcoal. His nostrils flare and he runs a hand over his curly head the way he does when he's agitated. Uncertain. "I promised Mr. Harrison I'd…" He trailed off. "Well, I owe it to him and—"

I take a step back, not liking his words. My hope shrivels. *Stupid, stupid girl.*

Declan's hand darts out and wraps around my wrist, pulling me up short. "I owe it to you, too. I promised I'd look out for you, and I did a piss poor job of that. Let me do right by you, by your family, Vivi. Don't marry Henry, or any other man, Genevieve. Marry me."

Declan's voice cracks on my full name and a pain I didn't know I still had the capability to feel rips through my chest. Heartache.

I thought he showed up because he cared. Because a part of him still…*wants* me, the way I always want him. But he's here because of a promise he made to Granddaddy.

I freeze, my body locking down under his touch. When did he make this promise to Granddaddy? When we were still in high school? Or, more recently? I know they never stopped talking. Is *this* what Granddaddy hoped to achieve with his marriage stipulation?

Before I can ask, Declan's eyes narrow, his expression fierce and unyielding. "I didn't fight for you the way I should have years ago. We swore we'd always be in each other's lives and…Vivi, I walked out of a game and drove right here because I wanted to see, for myself, if this was real." He jabs a finger in Henry's direction but doesn't look away. "And it's not. But what we once had…Jesus. Let me help, Vivi. Please."

My eyes burn as I war with my body to hold back the tears that are accumulating behind my nose, at the back of my throat. I can't blink. I can't look away. And I can't refute Declan's words because what we once had…was everything.

"Marry me, Vivi."

Heat unfurls in my chest, his words hypnotizing. They're layered in an apology I don't fully understand but I want it anyway. That summer, I pushed Declan away because I was hurting. Because even though we broke up, I found out only days after he flew to Dublin that I was pregnant with his baby. And then, I watched with horror as photos of him, drinking and partying with his arms slung around girls who weren't me popped up across social media. My heart broke and all the goodwill, all the feelings of friendship I convinced myself I could hang onto dissipated. Then, when I lost the baby…well, I lost a part of myself.

I clung to my hurt, to the unfairness of it all. I let that bitterness fuel my actions, keep me from answering Declan's phone calls, and refuse to see him when he came home to Nashville before leaving for college.

Declan coming here and making this demand of me, offering this strange sense of closure, is dizzying. It's fucked up and agonizing and…thrilling.

My stomach somersaults but I keep my face impassive, not wanting to let on how much his words affect me. How much he affects me.

"Genevieve, are you sure?" Henry asks.

I keep my eyes trained on Declan. His thumb traces my cheekbone and I'm captivated by the intensity of his gaze. Gray thunderclouds in a harsh, summer storm. "Be sure, Vivi," he murmurs.

Why is my heart rate increasing at his words? I know, firsthand, how easy Declan Yaeger's pretty words can fall flat.

It will always be me and you, Vivi. I will always come home to you.

Except he didn't. And now, it's for the wrong damn reason.

I shake the memory from my mind as Henry clears his throat.

"Father Ward," Declan bellows.

Father Ward shuffles back into the church, since I know he was just outside eavesdropping.

"I've come home to marry my Vivi. Today," Declan says clearly, pulling a gasp from my lips and a begrudgingly impressed chuckle from Henry. But Declan stares straight at me, right down to my soul, the only man who ever saw that deep, when he asks, "Will you marry me, Genevieve Rae?"

His thumb drops, swiping along my jaw, before stopping underneath my chin and tipping my face up to his.

I can't read anything in his gaze except that it's too much. Too full. Swirling, simmering emotions I don't fully understand.

"Vivi?" he asks, hurt wrapping around his tone.

Declan is my best option right now. If I want to keep Granddaddy's legacy going, if I want to continue doing good, meaningful work, then I need to marry him today.

I glance at Henry. I take in his amused, slightly concerned expression.

I let out a shaky exhale and make my decision.

At least with Declan, there's a history I can count on. I know he'll support my work. I know he won't expect me to dote on him. And I know, given all the baggage and hurt between us, that our relationship will never be more than this. More than a promise he made to Granddaddy and a legacy I vowed to protect. So, I grasp the St. Genevieve pendant hanging around my neck, open my mouth, and say the word I thought I'd always say to Declan, but never out of obligation. "Yes."

DECLAN and I are married an hour later to the surprised tears and cheers of our entire town. The scent of magnolias perfumes the church. A violin plays softly in the background. The pews are filled, the doors wide open, sunlight streaming in.

It's a perfect day for a wedding and mine is beautiful. A beautiful farce. Because I'm marrying a stranger, a man I don't know anymore even though he once held my heart in his hands. Right now, marrying Declan is the best way to safeguard Granddaddy's legacy, the mission of the foundation, and my life's purpose. So, I accept Alfred's begrudging best wishes, put on a brave smile, and walk down the aisle.

My wedding dress, an intricate number heavy with beading and layers upon layers of tulle, wraps around me like a protective cloak. My something old, a tiny locket that belonged to Mama, nestles against my heart, right next to Saint Genevieve, like a talisman. I wore it today for luck but now, in this moment, it seems much more than that.

It feels like Mama is watching over me, watching me marry the man who once ruled my heart, and whispering that it's all going to turn out okay. For a second in time, a heartbeat, a blink, I lose myself in Declan's eyes, my future melds with his, and the world stops.

If Mama had to witness any moment of my life, I'm happy it's this one.

"You may kiss the bride," Father Ward announces after Declan and I exchange the rings that Mrs. Cleary delivered to the church upon hearing the news.

Declan's hands find my waist and I suck in a breath, already dizzy from the rows of people staring at us, straining to catch a glimpse of our union, one built on past hurts and future hopes.

The corner of Declan's mouth quirks up. His eyes blaze, not with the confusion of earlier, but with a yearning I feel bone-deep. His lips part, my chin tips upward, and so slowly I can hear the pounding of my heart, we move. We lean toward each other, pulled by an invisible tug that always existed between us.

"Vivi," he breathes out, his words feathering over my lips. Then, his mouth is on mine, and I'm transported to the past.

Declan's lips are soft, at odds with the searching looks he's been shooting my way since I first saw him in the church. But I don't want to think about that right now. Right now, I want to savor this moment, since it won't happen again.

I kiss Declan to secure our marriage in front of our town. But his lips won't caress mine after this. His kiss is too dangerous, too potent. It has the power to make me believe in things I know aren't true. Like love and futures, like white houses on hills and baby giggles. Like all the plans we once dreamed up, when we were young and in love and so sweetly naïve.

But for right now, this one moment…

I close my eyes, I part my mouth, and I kiss Declan Yaeger the same way I did when I was twelve. With hope and heart and heat.

I also pull away first, noting the confusion swirling in his gaze, the frown moving over his face. Clasping his hand in mine, I turn toward our guests and raise our hands in the air, reveling in the joy that rings out, infusing the church with a happy glow I wish was real. Real enough to live in.

Henry places his hand over his heart and tips his head in my direction.

Alfred rolls his eyes, but I ignore him.

Instead, I lift my face toward the heavens and thank

Granddaddy for leaving me a legacy worth pursuing. No matter the cost.

CHAPTER 3
DECLAN

My wedding reception is fancier than I ever thought it would be. Not that I imagined my wedding much, but I never considered the possibility of a full waitstaff, band, and dancing under a springtime sky with little strands of lights glimmering like stars.

As I look around the Harrison Estate, draped in tents, with high-top tables and tea lights, I know that Vivi had a hand in all the planning. I also know that if anyone can pull together a wedding in a handful of days, it's her. The rustic elegance, the attention to details, the warmth of the space, it all has Vivi's touch stamped on it.

The only thing missing is my bride. Since Church, she's been distant toward me, putting space between us even as I tried to close it. I don't know what she's thinking. I have no clue what changed in the time between her kiss at the altar and sitting down to dinner, but something is off.

The Vivi I remember was outgoing and free-spirited. This version is much more reserved, even aloof. She's pretty and polite but doesn't exude the same boundless enthusiasm. Instead, she's almost…cautious.

I sigh, scoping the space until I locate her on the dance

floor. I didn't think I'd end the day as a husband, much less one in the doghouse.

"You're avoiding me." I pull Vivi into my arms for an obligatory dance.

Rumors have been circling from the second it became public knowledge that I was back in town. So far, Genevieve and I have done nothing to encourage or discourage them. We've soundlessly agreed to just let people think what they will.

"We're married now. I couldn't avoid you if I tried." She lifts her eyebrows, a teasing smirk on her lips.

I smile, somehow missing her even more now that I have her again. Or maybe I'm just acutely aware of all the missed years we lost?

"Why'd you say yes to me and not Henry? At the end, he was going to give in." It's a stupid question and I shouldn't ask it but the jealousy I felt when I saw Vivi earlier today, wrapped in a white wedding dress for another man, hasn't receded. If anything, it's only sharpened since I've realized how close I was to losing her completely. Why did it take me this long to come home? Why didn't I speak to her sooner? Is it because even though Mr. Harrison never provided details about her life, I always knew she was safe? And now, what? I've lost my only connection to her?

The nostalgia I feel for the past is sharp and I wonder what our life together will look like. Will she move to Boston? Will I split my time here? Will our marriage be… real?

And why doesn't the thought of it terrify the hell out of me?

"It's better for Henry this way," she replies as I twirl her.

My jaw snaps closed, irritated that her concern is still Henry. But I can't deny that her commitment to him, to their friendship, or whatever the hell is between them, impresses me. Their connection is deep enough that she would protect it by marrying me. It's the kind of connection, the type of trust, that Vivi and I used to share.

I dip her gently and she smiles up at me, her whole face brightening. It hits me that now, I don't have that type of relationship with anyone. Sure, the guys on my team have my back but there is no one in my life that would step up for me the way Vivi did for Henry.

The way she used to for me. Suddenly, my nostalgia aches. It crashes over me and I wish I could go back…in time. In life. To what was. Can it ever be that way again?

"What's wrong?" she asks softly as I pull her back up.

I shake my head, continuing our dance. "It's just, I didn't realize how much time…how much everything's changed."

"Here? In Nashville?"

I bite the corner of my mouth. "Between us."

Surprise washes over Vivi's expression. "Oh. I…"

I squeeze her hand. "You don't have to say anything. I don't think I'm even making sense. The past two days have been a whirlwind. It's just…being back is strange. In some ways, it feels like nothing's changed and in others, everything is different than I remember."

"We're not the same people anymore, Dec," she says quietly, using my old nickname. It pulls at the corner of my memory, unraveling a thousand other moments that Vivi and I shared.

"No, we're not," I agree. "But we *are* married now."

"Yes." She clears her throat, suddenly uncomfortable. "We'll have to talk about that." Uncertainty swims in her eyes and I stop, right in the middle of the dance floor, to try to decipher its cause when Alfred stops beside us.

"Your dad's on the phone," he tells Vivi. "He just got back to base, and this is his first call out. He didn't know about Granddaddy or…this." Alfred's eyes flick to mine before he turns back to Vivi. "He wants to speak to you."

"Of course," she says breezily, shooting me a smile that's

filled with relief. It causes a pang to cut through my chest because I recognize it. She used to flash it in high school, when she talked her way out of an algebra test, or at her Granddaddy, when he didn't call her out for missing curfew. But never has she turned it on me. Until now. *We're not the same people anymore, Dec.*

"Tell your dad I say hello. And sorry, that I didn't call for his blessing," I say, half joking. Vivi's daddy never recovered from the loss of his wife, who passed in childbirth with Vivi. Afterwards, he deployed to the Middle East and only came home to Tennessee occasionally. Instead, Vivi would meet him abroad, and they would have fun adventures away from the home his wife passed away in.

Vivi laughs but follows her cousin inside their granddaddy's home. I watch her go, wondering about the kind of life she leads now. Why didn't she go to college? Does she still live here, in her childhood home? Or does she rent a place downtown? Does she have a best friend besides Henry? Did she ever fall in love again?

Feeling bowled over by all the changes, I move to the edge of the dance floor.

"Here." Mrs. Cleary passes me her scotch.

"Thanks, Mrs. C." I raise the tumbler to my lips. Lord knows I need a drink. Or ten.

Today, I married Genevieve Rae, the love of my life. Even though I barely know her. Even though she's looking at me like I'm an item to be crossed off her checklist, instead of a man she once dreamed up a future with. Even though all the reasons sound wrong, something about being back with Vivi *feels* right. The whole thing is disconcerting, not to mention mentally exhausting on top of the physical fatigue that's starting to creep in.

I take a sip of the strong scotch and savor its taste. Smooth and bold. I pull out my phone and wince at the messages. They've been rolling in since I powered my phone back on.

Da. My team captain, Austin. Coach Phillips. Teammates and friends. Everyone wondering what the hell happened. What the hell I'm doing.

And I don't have an answer for any of them because I don't know. I look down at the gold band, a bit too tight since it was meant for Henry, that encircles my left ring finger. I married Genevieve. *Married.*

The thought of marriage hasn't crossed my mind once since I left this town in my rearview mirror. I spent all four years of college avoiding any kind of serious romantic entanglement. Other than a handful of summers, nights spent with Luca Pandatelli wingman-ing me, as we partied and blew off steam after I signed with the Hawks, I've mostly flown under the radar. I prefer to keep my private life…private. Discrete.

Now, I'll be on every damn internet gossip site in the country, with photos of my *marriage* to Genevieve out there for everyone to dissect. I married a woman I barely know. Not anymore.

We haven't shared more than a handful of sentences in seven years and now, she's my legal wife, and I'm not mad about it. In fact, a part of me feels relieved which makes no damn sense and messes with my mind even more.

"It's good to see you kids together again," Mrs. Cleary says from beside me.

I look at her friendly smile and chuckle. Does she really believe that Vivi and I are in love? Can we be again? For a moment, in the church today, I thought there was a chance, a spark, of something. But now…I just don't know.

The relief in Vivi's smile as she left the dance floor. The way she barely looked at me over dinner. Does she regret it?

But what was the alternative? Let her marry Henry? Or worse, a random man who isn't me? The thought makes me nauseous. I didn't stand a chance when I witnessed the dejection that ringed her irises when Henry tried to back out of their arrangement.

I hated that she was hurting. Hated more that she felt enough for Henry to protect him at the expense of herself. So, what did I do? Apparently, I opened Pandora's box. Because, other than the one moment in church, when she kissed me like I was oxygen, Vivi has treated me with polite detachment the entire evening.

She reenters the dance floor and Henry takes her in his arms. She tips her head back and laughs as he spins her. I toss back the scotch, let its heat warm the coldness traveling through my limbs and watch my wife give another man the sunbeam smile she won't give me.

My phone buzzes in my pocket and I close my eyes, knowing I can't ignore the messages forever. Besides, I can't bear to look at Genevieve anymore, not when she's dancing and smiling and talking like nothing's wrong. Like her wedding day is all she dreamed it would be even though her eyes are wary when they fall on her groom.

I pull out my phone and swear.

DA

Send me a photo, son. Abilene's reading me updates on some sports gossip website and I need proof! Are you happy?

AUSTIN

Did you just get married?

SIMS

Are you fucking high? Do you need help? Bro, I'm coming to fucking Tennessee.

JAMES

Yaeger, are you in trouble?

COACH

Monday morning. My office at 9 a.m. You better be ready to explain yourself.

PANDA

I hear congratulations are in order...

I wince at the messages and shame fills my gut at Coach's. I can't believe I walked out of the arena right before a game, leaving my team one guy short. Coach called up Keller to play in my position and there's no way in hell the rookie was ready.

Another message buzzes and this time, I snort, grateful to my teammate Easton's girl for always providing some comic relief.

EASTON

Yaeger, it's Claire. Dude, your wifey is gorgeous. Why'd you never tell me about her? I've always wanted a girlfriend (Indy doesn't really count because she's my cousin) with a Southern drawl. Also, East says congrats.

East hit the damn lottery with Claire. She's smart, feisty, and has a big heart...not unlike the woman now wearing my ring.

I glance up as Vivi walks toward me. "How are you holding up?"

"Fine," I say, slipping my phone back in my pocket.

She yawns. "You gettin' tired?"

I smirk. "Is that your way of telling me you are?"

She shrugs. "I can't exactly leave our wedding without you so..."

"Come on." I extend my hand and it's like I'm offering an olive branch.

Vivi places her hand in mine, and we walk away from the dance floor, now overflowing with guests, most of whom I don't recognize.

"I'm already packed." Vivi leads me toward her childhood

home, her granddaddy's mansion. "So I can head back to Boston with you."

"What? You want to…come home with me?" I trail the familiar path behind her, moments of my childhood colliding with my present, giving me a massive mind fuck.

Vivi used to sit under the big weeping willow tree and read for hours. Worn copies of *The Baby-Sitters Club* and *Nancy Drew* that once belonged to her mother. She used to sketch birds from the wraparound porch and hum lullabies. She used to fill the drafty halls with laughter and…energy.

We step into the house, and I stop short as the familiar scent I'd never be able to recall until this second, tobacco and leather and cedar, rolls over me. The rugs and tapestries are just as I remember them. The wainscotting in the formal dining room and the dated wallpaper Vivi and I used to poke fun at is still on the walls. The pride and joy of Beau Harrison wraps around us like a hug.

"I miss him," Vivi says quietly, her eyes trained on the framed photos on the mantle. Most of them are of her and Mr. Harrison. In many ways, he raised her. He was the constant she could count on.

I swallow past the unexpected emotion in my throat, suddenly wishing I checked in on him more. Wishing that I mailed the box with the signed hockey gear still sitting in my condo. Wishing our conversations centered more on him and his life instead of on me and hockey. I squeeze Vivi's hand. "He was a giant among men."

She nods, dropping her face to hide the emotion playing out across her expression. "He loved you. Like a son."

Her words pierce something deep inside because she says them with pride and not the hurt that I expected. She looks at me now, her blue eyes brimming with tears, her bottom lip quivering. "He watched all your games when you were a Gopher."

I snort at her reference of the University of Minnesota's mascot, Goldy.

"And then, when you signed with the Hawks, he was so unbelievably proud. Never missed a game."

"I mostly rode the bench," I point out.

She smirks. "You still suited up."

"We never lost touch," I tell her, wanting her to know that while I obviously fell out of her favor, I was able to hang onto it with Mr. Harrison.

"I know," she murmurs, the corner of her mouth curling upwards. "I just, I never asked about you because it was… hard."

My brows pull together. "Why, Vivi? What happened? When we decided to break up, we said—"

"I know," she cuts me off, tugging her hand out of mine. Her eyes shudder over, hardening. "But things change, Dec."

"*What* changed?" I press, not admitting how much that summer sucked. Hurt. Not only did I lose my girlfriend, but I lost my best friend too. And then I acted like a jackass, letting my cousins pull me all over Dublin, chugging pints of Guinness and tossing back whiskey, to dull the pain that went along with Vivi ignoring my phone calls and not responding to my messages. And then, when I came back for a few days before heading off to college, she refused to see me.

She cuts me a hard look, filled with a sadness I don't understand. "A lot."

I toss my hands up, exasperated. "Look, I know we grew up and our lives went in two different directions but Vivi, we're married now. We're going to stay married for at least…" I trail off, waiting for her to fill in the blank since I wasn't at the reading of Mr. Harrison's will.

"A year."

"A year," I repeat. That's it? That's all I'll have her for?

"I promise I won't make it difficult for you," she says and my gaze snaps back to hers.

"Difficult? What are you talking about?"

She shrugs. "Just that I know you have your own life and that you did me a favor by doing this." She points to her wedding band. "Come on," she says, abruptly ending our conversation, leaving it unresolved.

I follow her as she threads through the hallways. When I enter her bedroom, the tightness in my stomach eases. I'm plunged back into high school. The four-poster bed with the white eyelet cover is still in the corner. Her desk holds piles of neatly stacked books. Everything is tidy and in its place, just the way she likes it.

"I'm ready," she says, drawing my attention to the suitcase handle she's gripping and the bag over her shoulder.

"That's all you have? That's...it?"

"It's everything I need."

"Wait, are you planning to move permanently? To Boston?" I ask, dumbfounded.

Vivi chuckles. "Yeah, Declan. Usually, when two people marry, they live together. Unless...you don't want to?"

I shake my head, still unnerved by all these changes. "But your whole life is here," I rationalize, trying to process everything that's happened today. On top of a seventeen-hour drive and severe sleep withdrawal, I can't keep up with the changing events unfolding around me. I don't even know what's real anymore. "What about the foundation? Isn't it... here?"

Vivi nods. "Headquarters are. But I can work remote for the next few months and fly back as needed. One of the initiatives we're thinking about is to open a women's shelter. In the interim, I'd love to start collaborating with women's shelters in cities across the U.S. Did you know Boston has the first women's shelter?"

I shake my head.

"It's a good city to kick off this new program."

"Okay," I say, my gaze catching on an old photo of Vivi

and me. It's pinned in place on a corkboard above her desk. I'm wearing my hockey jersey from my high school travel team, my arm casually slung around her shoulders. She's smiling up at me, her eyes wide and adoring, her face open and beaming.

I finger the edge of the photo, wondering why she kept it up when all the other memories of us—photos, a framed poem I gave her on our first anniversary, stuffed animals won at carnivals, a corsage from prom—are obviously missing.

"I wanted a reminder," she says softly.

I turn to look at her, waiting for more. I need some explanations to make sense of how everything is so…different.

"Of the person I used to be," she adds, her voice so low I almost don't make out the words.

I frown, my mouth dropping open as a crushing sadness falls over her face. Tears well in her eyes and I step forward, but she holds out a hand.

"I'm okay," she murmurs, and I'm not sure if she's talking to me or herself. "I'm fine." She lets out a long exhale and straightens her posture. Looking at me, she says, "If it's okay with you, I'd like to stay at Mrs. Cleary's tonight."

I nod.

"And then, I'll go home with you to Boston. I'll be diving into work on Monday, and it will keep me busy, so I won't be in your way much. We can sync our calendars, so I'll know when you're traveling and vice versa. Given our history, we should do okay as roommates. Although, I gotta warn you, I'm not much of a cook." She looks at me expectantly.

The confusion that's been swimming in my veins all day mixes with my exhaustion. It blazes into a frustration that bursts out of my mouth in a question demanding a response. An actual answer instead of the deflection Vivi's been flipping my way. "What the hell happened to us, Genevieve?"

CHAPTER 4
VIVI

It's the genuine bewilderment in Declan's eyes that pulls something in my chest, drawing it too tight, squeezing it too hard, making it ache. I stare back at him, wishing I had the words to answer his question. But I don't. Not without sharing too much, giving away too much from that awful summer I've tried to forget.

The loss of our baby. The loss of him. The hurt and heartache of witnessing him, living his best life in Ireland, while I sobbed on the bathroom floor. All of it, combined, broke something inside of me. Something that encouraged me to defer college and throw myself into the work of the foundation. I swore I'd never put myself in a position like that again. I'd never make myself so vulnerable, so trusting, as to hurt that deeply.

Now, with Declan staring at me like he doesn't know me anymore, I ache in a different way. The rationalizations, the lies, I repeated to myself in church ring false. If I let myself, I'd fall for Declan Yaeger all over again, with everything between us, in a heartbeat. And that's a problem, because when our year is up and his promise to Granddaddy fulfilled, it will leave me hurt and broken all over again.

The pain I tried to hide all day by keeping my distance from Declan rises to the surface and I know it bleeds into my expression because his gaze softens. For a moment, I see the boy beneath the man. The one who learned how to swim beside me in the creek, the kid who used to make me laugh until my stomach ached, the boy who gave me my first kiss. He helped me find my footing in the world, the two of us figuring things out as they happened, two motherless kids in a world that spun too fast. We always shared a connection and now…I don't know how to tell him this. How do I tell him about the heartache I felt when we broke up, even though we both knew it was for the best? How do I tell him about the baby we lost? What would that achieve? If he knows, will he hate me, resent me, for keeping it from him? Especially now that we're married?

"Vivi, talk to me." He moves closer, his frustration leaving him as quickly as it swooped in. His fingers wrap around mine, his warmth steadies me, and I wish I possessed the strength to lean into him and let him hold me.

I wish I had the kind of courage to let him in, to trust him again. But I haven't let any man, other than Henry, get too close since Declan hugged me goodbye before boarding a flight to Dublin.

For the past seven years, I've had some fun, but I've mostly worked my ass off. I poured my hurt and heartache into impactful work that focused on the needs of others. My work kept me grounded, kept me moving forward, kept me safe from the romantic attachments I'm too scared to form.

But I can't tell Declan that. I can't admit that our relationship, from high school, was the last meaningful one I had. That every guy since never came close to him. That I don't dream up personal plans anymore or see myself married with the kids the way I once did. Even if I could confide in Declan, I wouldn't share it today.

Not now, considering the sacrifice he made only hours

ago. He married me so I can run the foundation, the way I see fit. The foundation is what I should focus on moving forward. It's the only way I'll survive the next year with Declan. If I don't throw myself into work, I'll lose myself to him and his touch all over again.

"Declan," I start, my voice more level than I feel. I take a deep breath and I lie. "We grew up. You went to college in Minnesota, and I stayed here. You became a hockey player and I thrived at the foundation. Our lives just went in two different directions. That's all. I know when we broke up we swore we'd be friends and it was a nice sentiment, but maybe too ambitious considering our ages and where we were at in our lives."

He frowns, his lips pursing in a silent question. *What the hell are you talking about?* But he doesn't voice it and I don't provide the answer. Instead, I charge on. "I appreciate what you did for me today, more than you realize. You've given me the means to continue the work of the foundation in the spirit my grandparents intended it. You've supported me in a way I'll never be able to repay—"

"You don't have to."

"The foundation is…well, it's my life now. This work is so important to me and carrying on Granddaddy's legacy means the world to me. And I guess, in a way, you held up a promise you felt honor bound to protect."

"Genevieve—"

"I have no idea why Granddaddy added the marriage stipulation to his will but, he did. Given our history, I think we should try for a friendship."

"Friendship," he says slowly.

"You'll have hockey and I'll have work and we'll be able to support each other's careers," I fumble through, my stomach twisting as his eyes narrow.

"That's all you want? *Friendship*?" he presses.

I clear my throat. "It's all I can handle."

Surprise causes his eyebrows to lift. "Why?"

I chuckle and drag my hand across my cheek. "I forgot how demanding you are."

"Persistent," he clarifies. "And only when I care to be."

"And you think this is a topic worth caring about?"

"You're always a topic I care about, Vivi."

I sigh, his words sweet but...alarming. "That's the problem, Dec. I can't...do more than this"—I gesture between us—"with you."

"Because we broke up?"

I bite my bottom lip and nod.

Whatever he reads in my expression causes his lips to roll together and his nostrils to flare. We stare at each other for several long moments, both trying to feel the other out, to get a pulse on the new dynamic between us.

"Okay," I change tactics. "How do you see this working out? Me and you?" I cross my arms over my chest.

He smirks, his eyes blazing with a challenge that excites and terrifies me. "Well, you'd obviously be naked in my bed—"

I gasp.

"Every single night," he laughs, making me blush. Then he shakes his head. "Hell, I don't know, Vivi. For one, we'd be able to talk about things."

"That's what we're doing now."

"Then why does it feel so...forced."

"Because we don't know each other anymore," I repeat.

"I guess not," he agrees, his expression bleak. "But you're moving to Boston."

"Yeah. And look, I know that we're both adults with lives and...needs." Heat blazes in my cheeks and Declan's jaw snaps closed. I force myself to soldier on, "So, if you can be discreet with women, I'd—"

"There'll be no women," he says with finality. His eyes are

so dark, I can't decipher between his iris and his pupil. He widens his stance, and his stare becomes a glare.

"I've offended you."

He swears. "Hell yeah, you've offended me, Vivi. What the hell did you think? That I'd offer to marry you and two days later, be messing around with some girls in Boston? I've never played games like that, and you know it. Not once, when we were together, did I ever give you the idea that I'd be unfaithful to you. Do you really think I've changed that much? That my values are so different now? That I'd break my damn marriage vows? To you?"

Shock rocks through me. I peer up at him, reading the seriousness in his gaze. Oh God, he means it. Those photos of him, drunk and eighteen, partying in pubs across Dublin, come to mind. But we weren't together then. In fact, I wasn't even speaking to him. I shake my head to clear it. The man standing here now isn't eighteen. He's twenty-six, my husband, and hurt at the accusation I insinuated.

The intensity of his anger checks some of my doubt and I release a shaky breath. "I don't know how to do this with you."

"Well, I've never been married before, either."

I wet my lips; my throat suddenly filled with sand. "I don't know how to trust you," I clarify, my voice cracking. "I haven't trusted any man but Henry in a long time."

Declan sighs, his eyes shuddering closed. His palm slides over his hair and he pulls at his curls. When he opens his eyes, I see the fatigue blaring from them. "Vivi, I haven't slept in two fucking days. When I heard you were marrying Henry, I drove straight here. I wanted to see you; I wanted answers. But now, all I have are questions. I never expected Henry to fucking jilt you, or for you to be okay with that."

I flush at the accusation in his tone.

"Mr. Harrison's gone. Everyone from town is shooting me these long side glances I don't understand. One minute, you're kissing me the way you used to and the next, you're essentially telling me that we're strangers. I know that we've changed, Vivi, but I didn't realize how much. I didn't expect to feel so damn confused."

As much as the words hurt to hear, they're true. I know I've changed; I told him as much. I dip my head in acknowledgment, which only serves to frustrate Declan more.

"This was a mistake," he mutters, yanking on his curls. It's such a Declan move, a reminder of the past, that I almost smile. But I catch myself at the last moment and stare at his broad shoulders instead. This mistake is my saving grace, but I guess from his perspective, a man who can have any woman he wants, marrying his high school sweetheart who's throwing out mixed signals would constitute a blunder in judgement.

"Dec—"

"It's okay," he cuts me off, scraping a hand over his face. "I just need to sleep. Let's just go, okay?" He takes my bag from my shoulder and grips my suitcase handle. "We can talk more about everything on the ride to Boston." He leads me down the dark corridor and outside.

We make a quick detour to say goodbye to our guests. I kiss Henry's cheeks in farewell and give Alfred a hug goodbye. Then, Declan ushers me into his SUV and drives away, putting distance between us and the twinkling lights.

I watch my home fade from view, remembering my beautiful childhood and all the memories I made with Granddaddy.

We turn a corner toward Mrs. Cleary's bed-and-breakfast and the house disappears.

I turn in my seat and let out a long exhale. From here on out, I'm only looking forward.

WHEN WE ENTER his room at Mrs. Cleary's, he locks the door behind us and looks me over. I fidget nervously at the foot of the bed, wondering how the hell I'm supposed to sleep next to him with so much unresolved baggage between us. So far, we haven't even managed to conclude a conversation.

Now, in the small room, I feel the confusion Declan spoke about. Because it feels awkward, the two of us, in here together. Even though he's the only man I've ever truly loved, I don't know how to act around him. How am I supposed to sleep next to him? Will his skin brush against mine? Will he reach out and place his hand on my hip the way he used to?

Today, at the church, I kissed him on my terms. There's no way I can handle him touching me on his. I'll analyze his intentions too much. I'll do all the things I swore to myself in church today that I wouldn't.

But who am I kidding? Declan's always managed to make me feel more than I want to. I'm already confiding in him more than I intended.

It's been seven years and still, I haven't moved on. Lord knows I've tried but after Declan, it was easier to keep my romantic entanglements low-key and fun. A series of first or fifth dates that were always of the moment but never more. Yeah, I've had sex and gotten drunk and done a bunch of things a normal college kid checks off her bucket list. I just did them without the college part. I never rushed a sorority, but I went to frat parties at Vanderbilt. I perfected my keg stand. I hooked up with a few football players and rocked their jerseys. They called me sweetheart or beautiful and we had sex, but I never felt half of what I did with Declan. I never orgasmed or exchanged "I love you's." In fact, I rarely even hooked up sober.

And that concluded my experience. I never made the strong female friendships most of my peers have. I never agonized over changing my major or tuition costs. Instead, I worked. I proposed new programs at the foundation. I lived in Granddaddy's home. And I tried to fill up my empty with good deeds.

"I'll take the floor," Declan sighs, tugging a pillow from the bed.

Shit. Guilt expands in my stomach. He looks haggard, as if he's going to collapse from exhaustion.

"No." I reach out, placing my hand on his wrist. "It's fine." He looks at me, really studies me. I nudge him toward the bed. "You need to sleep, Declan. Go on."

He sits down on the edge of the bed and pulls off his shoes. Then he stuffs the pillow behind his head and lays back. "You sure?"

"Yeah."

"I'll sleep on top of the comforter."

At the sincerity in his tone, an unexpected rush of tears surges forward. He knows I'm uncertain. He can still read me. And knowing that I feel awkward, he's doing his best to put me at ease. Even now that I've made a mess of his life and his future. The one he worked so hard to build, the one that made Granddaddy's eyes twinkle.

God, what is wrong with me? How could I marry Declan Yaeger? How could I legally tie myself to him and think this was a situation I could handle? Leave unscathed? I'm still healing from his first heartbreak.

"Stop thinking and come sleep, Vivi." He yanks me from my thoughts, his voice thick with sleep. "We'll hash it out tomorrow."

"Promise?"

A soft smile curls his lips, but he doesn't open his eyes. "Promise, babe."

"Okay," I say, before I head into the bathroom. I pull the

pins from my hair until it tumbles down, a waterfall of blonde waves. I scrub the makeup from my face until my skin is clean and the freckles on the bridge of my nose stand out, prominent.

I unzip my wedding dress and let it pool around my feet. Picking it up, I toss it over the shower door. Then I turn and stare at my reflection in the mirror. I lean close and give myself a stern talking to.

"Genevieve Rae, you got this. It's one year of marriage, that's it. Keep your heart on lock and focus on the work. On the foundation. Now is not the time to get stuck in the past, to get hung up on what-ifs or things that never came to fruition. Declan is a man, with a life, and a future. You're just a part of his past, a promise he wants to keep. That's it."

I give myself a severe look to solidify my words, pull on my pajamas, and exit the bathroom.

Declan's light snore fills the space and I smile. I tiptoe to my side of the bed and sit down, watching the beautiful man beside me sleep, his breathing even, his body relaxed. His face is serene, pursed lips that once tasted every inch of my skin, and dark eyelashes I used to enviously tease him about.

Declan Yaeger grew up to dazzle, the way I always knew he would.

And now, he's my husband.

The thought causes a wave of insecurity, uncertainty, to roll through me. What will he think if he knows about the miscarriage? What will he think if he learns of my past, the secret I've kept from him? It's only supposed to be one year, and already, our marriage seems like it won't last that long. How can it? With so many knots to untie. With a complicated history and messy feelings, between us?

I look down at my ring finger. My thumb runs along the dainty, gold band.

I used to think Declan would become my husband. But never like this.

CHAPTER 5
DECLAN

"I got you a coffee. Two sugars." Vivi places a mug on the bedside table as I pull myself into a seated position.

I drag my palm over my face, wincing when I realize I need to shave. How many days has it been since I left Boston? I glance down at my dress pants and bare feet. The gold ring on my left hand catches my eye and everything from yesterday comes barreling back.

"We got married," I state, glancing up at Genevieve.

She chuckles and nods, her golden hair rushing forward. Her face is bare now, clear from all the makeup she was wearing yesterday, and she looks younger. More like the woman I first fell in love with. Her blue eyes bore into mine, guarded, but warm. Christ, she's something else all right.

She scratches at her cheek. "Do I have something on my face?"

I shake my head. "No, it's just, you're beautiful."

She blushes and sits down in the chair across from the bed, angling her body toward mine.

I pick up the coffee and blow on it before taking a sip. "Thanks for the caffeine."

"You had a long drive."

"Yesterday was a long day." I study Vivi over the rim of my cup. Of course, she grew into a stunning woman. But more than that, she stayed true to herself. She's still a compassionate, considerate, kind person who continues to put the needs of others first. "I know you keep saying you've changed—"

She looks up sharply.

"But from where I'm sitting, you're still the girl who wanted to open a public library, bead bracelets, and dance with butterflies. I still see the person I remember."

She smiles, giving me that sunbeam that could solar power the planet. I grin back.

"You remember that?" she asks, quietly.

"I remember everything, Vivi. I just don't understand it all."

At my words, she clams back up and I mentally curse myself.

She stands from her perch on the chair. "We should pack up and get out of here. It's a long drive back."

"Yeah," I agree, forcing myself to stand from the creaking bed. "You need to do anything before we roll out?"

"Just check in with work." She shakes her phone at me before dipping into the hallway.

I stare at the closed door behind her, wondering if things will ever feel natural between us again. There have been moments, minutes even, where it's me and Vivi again. But other times, like now, things between us are stifled and awkward. What happened the summer I left? Why did she stop taking my calls? Why would she refuse to see me before I left for college?

And why didn't I bother to find out?

VIVI FALLS ASLEEP an hour into our drive and I'm relieved. Mostly because I feel guilty and frustrated, out of my depth and confused. It's strange, having nothing to say to the woman I used to talk to for hours. It drives home how much time has passed, how much we don't know each other now.

In sleep, she looks more like the girl I remember. Her brow, constantly pinched, smooths out. Her lips purse thoughtfully. Her eyelashes flutter along the tops of her cheeks. She looks like an angel, peaceful and sweet.

I smile over at her, parts of our past, half-forgotten memories, flaring back to life. Jumping in the creek behind the Harrison Estate. Listening to Vivi play her piano, accompanied by Mr. Harrison on the harmonica. The way he'd spin her up in his arms when she had a good report card.

He came to all my hockey games when he was in town, cheering louder than any of the parents in the stands. He was so proud of me when I earned a hockey scholarship that his eyes shimmered with emotion. And then, our conversation from just a few weeks ago.

"I won't be here forever, Declan."

"Ah, you got at least twenty more good years," I joked.

He laughed. "Yeah, I know. But just in case I'm not, I need you to do something for me."

"Anything."

"Take care of her. Vivi. She feels too deeply, cares too much, and when I'm gone, I'm worried she'll bury herself in work and forget to live."

Surprise had rocked through me because it's the most he's shared about Vivi in years. So, she works a lot? I wanted to ask more, to learn about her, but sticking to our unspoken agreement to not speak about Vivi, I cleared my throat. "She doing okay?"

"For now. But when I'm not here…"

"I swear it, Mr. Harrison." I gave my word.

But damn, I doubt he meant marry her. Unless…

Why the hell did he include that marriage stipulation? He wasn't old-fashioned by any means. He always encouraged Vivi to pursue the life she wanted. In fact, when we were kids, he often applauded her for how cleverly she outmaneuvered Henry and me in climbing trees or swimming laps. So, why would he want her to marry? Why would he call me that day? Something still doesn't add up and without Mr. Harrison here to answer my questions, I doubt I'll ever know the full story.

My phone rings and I glance at the console as Da's name pops up.

I answer through the Bluetooth. "Da."

"I guess congratulations are in order."

I grin and shake my head. "I don't know what came over me."

"I do. You love her," he says simply.

Of course I love her. But do I know her?

I don't know how to trust you. Those aren't wedding night words.

I look over at Vivi, all soft skin and sweetness.

"She's sleeping," I say and Da chuckles.

"Are you driving home?"

"Yes. Another…fifteen hours to go."

"Be careful, Declan. You didn't sleep enough."

"Don't I know it," I agree, picking my third coffee up from the center console and taking a swig.

"Have you heard from the team?"

I sigh. "Yeah, I'm meeting with Coach tomorrow."

"I don't envy the position you're in."

"Thanks," I say, sarcastically. "You know this is your fault right."

He snickers. "My fault? You should be thanking me."

"Yeah, yeah. Well, you've got a daughter-in-law now."

"Genevieve's always been like a daughter to me," Da

replies. "And I always knew you two would end up together."

"That makes one of us. I can't believe she and Henry…"

"He's a good man."

"He was gonna leave her at the damn altar." Anger laces my words because as much as I hate the thought of Henry marrying Genevieve, I also hate the fact that he let her down. Especially since she obviously *trusts* him.

"Maybe, but he and Vivi have been friends for a long time," Da says quietly.

I roll my eyes. "You moved back to Ireland when I left Tennessee. How do you know so much about Vivi and Henry's relationship?" The moment I say the words, I know the answer. "Mrs. Stevens."

"We kept in touch."

"And?" I press, annoyed. What isn't he telling me? Why does he know things about Vivi that he never shared with me?

"And Genevieve and Henry are best friends. They have been for a long time. Don't judge a relationship you know nothing about, son."

I bite my tongue because he's right. I'm just bothered because I don't understand their friendship. That and I hate feeling like the third wheel when that role used to be Henry's.

I swear, placing my coffee down so I can pinch the back of my neck, my fingers twisting in my curly hair. At times like these, when Da and I are physically so far apart, the distance seems even greater.

"Da, do you think I made a mistake?"

"Do you?"

I roll my eyes. "Don't try some psychology shit with me. I'm asking for your opinion."

"No, I don't think you made a mistake. I think you've been in love with Genevieve since you were ten and never had to work hard at it. With her, or with any other woman.

You're used to things being easy, Declan. You're used to having them go your way. Now, you're married and…"

"And?"

"Marriage takes work. You need to trust each other, communicate, grow together."

"I married a woman I barely know and—"

"You know Viv."

I sigh, exasperated.

"You do," he says. "You know the parts of her that matter. You know her heart. To learn the rest, you need to give her the time to trust you."

"What the hell did I ever do to lose Vivi's trust? She broke up with me, remember? What about me trusting her?"

"You both have a lot to work through. And now, that you're married, you'll both have to put in the work. It's not going to be easy, Declan. But the connection you and that girl have…well, if you can make it work, it will be worth it."

"Right," I say sarcastically, thinking about our one-year marriage, centered on friendship.

"She's a good woman, Declan. Give her a chance."

I grip the steering wheel tighter but mutter my agreement.

"I'm heading to Cork to see Abilene and the kids," Da changes the subject.

We chat about my aunt and cousins for a few minutes before ending our call. Next to me, Genevieve is still asleep. I'm not sure if her sleeping through our first day of marriage is a disappointment or a relief. I'm not sure of anything except the meeting reminder that pops up on my phone.

Tomorrow morning. Nine a.m. With Coach Phillips.

EVEN THOUGH WE promised to talk, we don't discuss anything serious. For seventeen long hours, we sit in states of silence or forced small talk.

Vivi is reserved, withdrawn. With each mile that ticks by, I find my confusion growing. It's late when we return to Boston and my weariness is bone level. For the second night in a row, I pass out on top of the bed covers, fully clothed. Vivi sleeps in my guest room, putting as much distance between us as possible while still being in the same condo.

My alarm goes off at seven a.m. and I drag myself from bed, feeling like I didn't sleep at all. My head spins, foggy and overtired. My body is sore, like I worked out instead of sitting in a car for thirty-five hours over the weekend.

I peek into my spare bedroom, posting up against the doorframe to watch Vivi sleep. She's tired too, her hair fanning out over the pillow. She's been quiet since we left Tennessee, a quietness that borders on desolate.

I know we need time to sort things out, to settle into our new normal. But her evasiveness is alarming. Having her here, with me, is confusing and agitating. I don't know how to act, what to say, or how to just be when she's around.

I pull the door to her bedroom closed as if the action will cut her off from my morning routine. It kind of does. I shower quickly, dress for my meeting with Coach, and slip outside before she wakes up.

Then, I point my SUV in the direction of The Meadows and mentally prepare myself for the verbal lashing that's coming. Will Coach bench me? Suspend me? End my career?

It's unheard of for a player about to take the ice to disappear. To leave the team hanging without so much as a word. Shame fills me as I think about how angry my teammates must have been, how disappointed Coach must feel. And then, to learn that I got married. What are they all going to think of me? Will they question my commitment to the season, to the Hawks?

For the first time since I raced out of The Meadows, fear for my career takes root. Did I really jeopardize everything I worked for to marry Vivi on a whim?

Take care of her.

I swear it.

Or did I fulfill a promise to the man who shaped me just as much as Da?

I don't know how to trust you.

Or did I take the first step in trying to win back the heart of the woman I've never stopped loving?

I sigh and park my SUV in front of The Meadows. I stop for a quick cup of coffee, the caffeine a necessity after this weekend, and make my way to Coach Phillip's office.

"Come in," he calls out after I knock.

When I push inside, Coach and Austin's grim faces meet mine.

"How was your wedding?" Coach asks and my stomach drops.

I close the door behind me and sit in the chair beside Austin. "I'm sorry."

Coach shakes his head and Austin mutters something under his breath.

"What the hell were you thinking, Yaeger? Leaving like that? We thought...I don't know what we thought. That you were in some kind of trouble," Austin bites out.

"Your behavior was unprofessional and immature. You can't just leave your team hanging, cut out because your girlfriend's got drama." Coach leans forward in his chair, his eyes leveling me over his desk.

I swallow but remain silent. Whatever they say right now, they're entitled to, and I'd be a pussy if I tried to flip bullshit rationalizations to explain my behavior. The truth is, I was wrong. And I went about everything the wrong way.

"Are you suspending me?" I ask.

Coach shakes his head and Austin glares at me.

"We need you, Yaeger. The team needs you," Austin says. "We're having a good season but the next few games…"

"I'll be there. All in," I swear.

"Why didn't you tell anyone you were engaged?" Coach asks, steepling his hands. Coach Phillips is often quiet but since I spent my first seasons with the Hawks riding the bench, I've had ample opportunities to witness just how observant he is.

"I'm not going to sit here and spit bullshit or try to make sense of my actions. But I wasn't engaged. The whole weekend was…a family emergency of sorts. Something I needed to do that I don't think anyone would really understand. I know I handled it wrong and for that, I'm sorry. I never meant to let the team down or disappoint either of you." I look them both in the eye. "But my marriage isn't something I'm willing to discuss openly. All anyone needs to know is that it happened. Genevieve is my wife, and I won't miss another hockey game."

Coach's look is hard but after a moment he nods and flicks his wrist toward the door. "You're dismissed. Practice starts in an hour."

"Thank you, Coach."

"Yaeger," he says when I wrap my hand around the doorknob.

I look at him over my shoulder.

Coach points at me. "Pull a stunt like that again and you'll ride the bench for the duration of your contract."

"I understand." I pull open the door and slip into the hallway, relief flowing through my veins.

Knowing that my career isn't about to get squashed, I wonder how hockey and married life will coexist. Will Vivi come to my games? Will she sit with the other wives and girlfriends in the family box? Will she rock my jersey and cheer my name the way she used to, sitting next to Mr. Harrison and beaming at me?

I chuckle at myself as I push into the locker room. First, I need to get her to open up, to talk to me, to clue me in on what the hell happened that summer. Did she cut me off like that because we broke up? It was her idea! But now isn't the time to get lost down memory lane, trying to make sense of the past seven years in the making.

Now is the time to get my head on straight and focus on hockey. My career, my future, depends on it, since I obviously can't count on Genevieve.

CHAPTER 6
VIVI

I snort and roll my eyes at my friend's message. Henry's been sending a variation of the same text every morning since I married Declan a week ago. Each day, he inquires on our status, convinced that Dec and I are going to fall back into bed together.

I send off the message, unsurprised when my phone rings a moment later.

"You know I'm not a virgin, right?" I greet him.

He snickers. "I meant celibacy with Declan. I never thought you'd last this long."

My mouth drops open and I sputter.

"Oh please," Henry laughs. "You didn't think you'd last this long either."

I laugh with him. "I'm protecting myself."

"From what? He doesn't strike me as the type to have an STD."

I roll my eyes. "My heart, Henry. I'm protecting my heart."

"Keep telling yourself that, Viv. But your heart has been hung up on Declan since we were kids. All you're achieving now is high levels of sexual frustration, which can't be good for your health."

"Thanks for looking out," I quip.

"That's what friends are for."

"Did you tell your dad yet?" I repeat my text message aloud.

"Did you tell Declan yet?"

I swear. "Can't we talk about you now?"

"Not until we're done talking about you."

I laugh. "Henry!"

"Stop deflecting. I'm worried about you." The concern in his tone causes me to pause.

"I'm fine."

"You still love him. You need to tell him the truth. This year, your marriage together, it could be a second chance for you guys."

"I don't think I can handle that," I say quietly, not admitting that Declan alluded to as much too.

"Viv, you've never got closure from that summer. Now, you and Declan are married, you're living together, you're… you guys again."

"No, we're not."

"But you could be. You're holding yourself back."

"Maybe. But if I put myself out there and it doesn't work…" I trail off, unable to think of that scenario. Because it will crush me. Losing Declan once was enough to last a lifetime.

"What if it does?" Henry persists.

I sigh. "Can we talk about you now?"

He snorts. "Yeah, sure. No, I haven't told him. Mac came over for dinner last night, but I introduced him as my friend."

"Your mom is the best secret keeper."

"Tell me about it," he agrees.

Mrs. S is one hell of a confidant. Without a mom to confide in, I often sought out the advice of Henry's mom when I was growing up. She always offered a hot cup of tea, a tin of homemade oatmeal raisin cookies, and a shoulder to cry on. Other than Henry, she's the only person who knows of my miscarriage. There's no way she would out Henry to his father before he was ready.

"Listen, Viv, I really am sorry about the wedding. Part of the reason why I want you and Declan to hook up is to ease the guilt I feel for not going through with the marriage. For basically leaving you with no option *but* to marry Declan. And if you're not comfortable with him, then I feel even worse."

"Your honesty is always refreshing, my friend."

He snickers.

"But I'm the one who feels guilty. I never should have asked so much of you. And I'm not uncomfortable around Declan, not like that. I'm just, feeling things out. Everything is so new and while I'm trying to establish a friendship, he's looking at me like we could be more than that. Like he doesn't understand what happened to us in the first place."

"He probably doesn't. That's why you should tell him."

"And what if he hates me? Then I'm married to a guy who can't stand me instead of a man who just doesn't know what to make of me."

Henry scoffs. "Some choice. Declan could never hate you. Trust me."

"I do," I tell him the truth. "You're a good friend, Henry."

"I essentially left you at the altar, Genevieve." Apology coats his words. "I hate that I didn't step up when you needed me. But I'm glad Declan did. You've always been more than a friend to me. You've always been like my little sister. Since that first day Declan and I met you…"

An image of the creek with the warped rope we used to swing off of comes to life in my mind. Sunshine and cold water and enough laughter to fill even the bleakest of days. "I remember. How's Mac? How was dinner?"

"Good." I hear the smile in his voice. "He's really good, Viv. And dinner was…normal. It was nice."

"I'm happy to hear it."

"How's work going? Now that you're one-hundred percent in charge."

"It's only been a week. But it's been great. We're going to continue with all the programs we're currently running but all of our new outreach will be centered on women's shelters."

"And you're kicking that off in Boston?"

"Yes. It turned out to be symbolic. The first women's shelter started here in the 1970s."

"Kismet."

"We'll see. I'm excited to start. And, big surprise here, but Alfred offered to allot a percentage of profit from the lumber business to expanding the foundation's mission."

"Plot. Twist. Wow, I didn't think Alfred had it in him."

"I know, right? But it was a nice gesture. And it got me thinking, maybe we could start our own women's shelter here. Build it from the ground up. If I pull that off, you'll come to the opening, right?"

"Wouldn't miss it, babe."

The kettle begins to whistle on the stove. "I gotta go. Love you, Henry. Thanks for calling."

"Take care of yourself, Viv. Talk tomorrow."

I smile, knowing he'll keep checking up on me. "'Bye." I place the phone down and head to the stove, grabbing a mug from the cabinet, when a voice rings out behind me.

"You love him, huh?"

I whirl around, my hand flying to my throat. "Jesus, Declan. You scared me."

He lifts an eyebrow. "I live here," he says like I don't know that.

"I know. I just, I wasn't expecting you to be back so early."

He crosses his arms. "We still haven't talked, Vivi."

I sigh. "Would you like a tea?"

"No, Vivi," he growls, "I don't want a goddamn tea. I want you to talk to me. To let me in. To…not be strangers living in the same condo with wedding bands on our fingers."

I gulp, knowing that I've been avoiding him and this conversation. But Henry is right, I can't keep deflecting. At some point, I need to let Declan in. "Okay." I drop the teabag in my mug and pour out the water, the process soothing since it reminds me of Mrs. S and our chats.

Declan sits down at the kitchen table, leaning back in his chair until he's balancing on the back legs. "I want to know what the deal is with you and Henry. Why are you spouting off declarations of love for a man who left you hanging at the altar?"

My mouth drops open. "Were you…eavesdropping?"

He pinches the bridge of his nose before glaring at me. "Yeah, Vivi. I was skulking around my own condo, trying to listen to your conversation as you went on and on in the goddamn kitchen."

I shake my head. "Unbelievable."

"What?" He crosses his arms over his chest.

"You're jealous," I spit out, the realization loud in my mind.

Declan laughs, tossing his arms in the air. "Of course I'm jealous, Vivi. How can I not be? I married you so you could fulfill your life's purpose, so you could protect Mr. Harrison's legacy. I've spent the past week trying to reconnect with you, to talk to you, and you've shut me down every time. And now, I find you joking around with Henry, the guy who didn't step up for you when I did, and you think that wouldn't bother me?"

"You're right," I murmur, knowing that I've been unfair. "The truth is…" I bite my bottom lip and fiddle with the tag on the teabag. "The truth is that that summer was hard. Things changed, things happened—"

"What things?" he demands. "Why didn't you go to college? You were all set to attend Clemson, to rush Kappa Kappa Gamma, remember?"

I smile that he remembers the name of Mama's sorority. I always planned to follow in her footsteps and then… "I deferred. It was only supposed to be for a year but then, I got so caught up in the foundation's work and I didn't want to go anymore."

"You always wanted to make a circle of girlfriends."

"That's true. I hated always being the little rich girl in our town. If it wasn't for you and Henry, I wouldn't have had any true childhood friendships."

Dec lifts his eyebrows. "So, what changed? Why did you defer?"

I look at him and the longer I stare, the more memories from my past cloud my mind. Tears fill my eyes and I pinch the handle of my mug. I have to tell him; I know I do. But it's not the right time. We haven't built trust back between us. When we're together, we're still walking a tightrope, trying to find our balance with each other.

"Things I'm not ready to talk about," I mutter quietly.

Declan's stare hardens and then, horror washes over his face. He stands so quickly that the chair tips over. "Did someone hurt you?"

I wince, closing my eyes and shaking my head. "No, no nothing like that."

Declan swears and my eyes pop open.

He steps toward me, his hands wrapping around my

upper arms. He holds on to me tightly as he gazes into my eyes. His expression is fierce. "Vivi"—his tone is urgent—"you can tell me. If someone—"

"No one hurt me. I had a miscarriage," I blurt out the secret, the confession I've kept from him all these years.

Declan releases me like I've burned him. He staggers back, until his lower back collides with the kitchen counter. "Wh-what?"

"That summer…" I struggle to find the words. My hands tremble and uneasiness rolls through me. I'm in uncharted territory and I don't know what to say. I take a deep breath and tuck my hair behind my ears. "I found out two days after you left for Ireland that I was pregnant."

"And you didn't tell me?" he asks, his tone laced with hurt. His eyes narrow in betrayal. "Why, why the hell would you keep that from me?"

"Because I was terrified!" I shout at him, throwing a hand in his direction. "We broke up—"

"I was still in love with you!" he yells back, smacking a palm over his chest.

"Yeah? Would you have given up your hockey scholarship? Your dream? Would you have stayed in Tennessee to be a father?"

"I—" he falters, at a complete loss.

"I didn't know how to tell you. I was figuring everything out, thinking of the best way to break the news and not have you resent the hell out of me or feel like I was ruining your dream—"

"I'd never feel that way."

"And then I saw the pictures."

"What pictures?" His expression twists, confused.

I chuckle, the sound harsh. "Seriously? You were partying across Dublin. You were tagged every night drinking whiskey, chugging pints, doing stupid dares with your cousins. And…there were tons of girls."

"Girls?"

"With their arms around you, kissing your cheeks, sitting in your lap." The images flip through my mind, grainy photographs with streaks of light, fumbling hands. Wide smiles and hazy eyes.

Declan steps toward me. He looks stricken, his eyes now pleading. "Genevieve, I was so fucking heartbroken that we broke up. I knew we needed to; I knew college was going to be a whole different game. But that doesn't mean that I got on a plane and forgot about you. I called you every day and when you didn't answer, I acted like an idiot eighteen-year-old, pining for his ex-girlfriend, and let my cousins drag me out every night."

"So, you didn't hook up with anyone, for the whole summer?" I ask, even though I know I shouldn't. I'm not going to like the answer and I'm setting us both up for disappointment. But now, the question is out there, and I can't take it back.

Declan averts his gaze and my stomach coils into a knot.

"One night. I was drunk out of my mind and to be honest, I don't remember it. But the next morning...fuck." He yanks on the back of his hair. "It was stupid. It was a mistake. And I felt guilty as fuck the next morning. That's why I flew back early for a few days before college. And then, when you wouldn't see me, I went off to school pissed at you. How could you shut me out like that? Guess now I know..." Disappointment hangs heavy in his tone. His eyes are dark, brimming with a pain that I placed there.

It's hard to swallow as emotions I thought I had dealt with flood forward, clogging my throat.

"Declan," I whisper.

"I would have been here for you, Vivi. In a heartbeat. I would have come home." He rights his chair and sits back in it, staring at me across the table.

"I know."

"When did you miscarry?" His voice breaks on the word and my tears tip over, dropping onto my cheeks.

Declan moves his chair closer to mine and takes my hand in his, his thumb swiping over my knuckles as I drag the back of my hand across my cheek.

"Three weeks after you left. I was nine weeks pregnant. It's common in the first trimester. At least, that's what Mrs. Stevens told me."

"You told her?"

I shrug. "I didn't have anyone else I could confide in."

"So, Henry knows?"

I nod.

"That explains a lot," he mutters.

"What's that supposed to mean?" I bite out, not liking his tone.

But when he meets my gaze, I see the hurt in his eyes. "It means what I said. I didn't mean it as a dig. I just, I get why you guys are so close now."

"We really are best friends."

"Yeah," he agrees. "I'm happy you had him, and his family, to support you through that."

I pull my hand from Declan's and curl my fingers into the hem of my shirt, feeling vulnerable. Exposed. "Thanks."

Declan blows out a sigh. "Were you okay? Afterwards?"

I shake my head. "Not really. I was depressed. I stopped seeing the few girls from high school I kept in touch with. I deferred college. I kept to myself unless Henry dragged me to a frat party at Vanderbilt. Then, Granddaddy offered me a job and…I threw myself into it. The foundation became everything to me and to be honest, it's the only thing I had. For a long time, it's the only reason I got out of bed in the morning."

Anguish fills Declan's expression, deepening the lines between his eyes. His jaw is so tight I can hear his molars grind together. "Jesus," he murmurs, shaking his head. "I'm so fucking sorry, Vivi. I'm sorry I wasn't there for you. Not the way you needed."

"I'm sorry I didn't tell you the truth. But I couldn't face you after I lost the baby. I didn't know what to say and I didn't want you to leave for Minnesota hating me. Not any more than you already did."

"I could never hate you, babe," he says, his expression fierce. Sincere.

"I kind of just wanted to put it all behind me, you know? Thinking about it hurt, dwelling on it, on you, hurt and I just wanted a clean slate."

"I get that," he murmurs. "Is that why you ignored my calls?"

"Yes." I look at him when I say it; he deserves that much.

Declan continues to watch me but doesn't say anything. We sit in silence for a few moments. My tea grows cold. And then… "Did Mr. Harrison know?"

I freeze, wondering, for the first time, if Granddaddy knew all that I lost that summer. I certainly moped around but that could have been because Declan and I broke up. "I'm not sure," I say slowly. "He may have suspected. You know, he only added the marriage stipulation two weeks before he passed."

Declan's eyes widen and his lips part, surprised. "Two weeks?"

"Yeah." I narrow my eyes at his expression. "Why?"

He shakes his head and smirks at me. "You think we can do this, Vivi?"

"Be friends?" I ask cautiously.

Dec shakes his head. "No, be us."

"Us? Like…how we used to be?" My heart races at the thought. At the possibility.

"Yeah. You think you could…give me another chance."

I gape at him. "You *want* another chance? After everything I just told you?"

His smirk turns into a smile. "Vivi, I know what I said in church. And it's true, your granddaddy meant the world to me, and I'd do anything for him. But you know me. Do you really think, believe, that I'd marry you, *marry you*, because of a promise to your granddaddy?"

The air crackles to life, humming around me. The truth pulses between Declan and me, strewn in morsels and half-swallowed apologies across the kitchen table. I wrap my hands around my mug, focusing on the smooth ceramic that presses into my palms.

Declan looks at me expectantly, the charming smile I used to adore on his lips.

"No," I breathe out, knowing damn well that no one ever makes Declan Yaeger do something he doesn't want to.

"I married you because I want you, Vivi. I never stopped. And I still want you, even knowing why you pushed me away. Maybe even more now because I fucking hate that you went through that on your own. Baby, we can take it slow. We can go at whatever pace you're comfortable with. Take things one day at a time. And if after a year, you're not in love with me, I'll let you go, Vivi. But know that this year, I'm going to try my damnedest to fix the broken between us. To earn your love again."

CHAPTER 7
DECLAN

The weight plates rattle together as I slip the bar back in its holder and sit up on the bench. Swiping up a towel, I mop the sweat from my hair. My arms are fatigued and still, I want to push myself.

I want to just keep going, running, working out until Vivi's confession isn't looping in my mind. What was I thinking? Not getting an explanation all those years ago? Of course she was hurt. While I was partying in Dublin, she was mourning the loss of our baby. And yeah, a part of me is pissed that she didn't tell me she was pregnant. But a larger part of me is furious that I didn't fight for her when the Vivi I knew, the girl I loved, never would have blown me off like that. Not unless something happened. And learning you're pregnant, only to miscarry, is a big fucking something.

But I want her back. I want to deserve her heart the way I used to. I want her to truly be my wife.

The thought of losing her fires me up all over again and I move onto the leg machine, sitting down to do leg presses. My body aches, my muscles on fire, but my head is all over the place.

My old life doesn't make sense anymore. I don't recognize

the guy I was just two weeks ago, when I had a routine and total peace of mind. I can't get that ease back now even if I wanted it. And the strange thing is, I don't. I want Vivi, even with the hurt between us. I want her just as much as the day we broke up.

"You're going to burn out," Noah Scotch, one of the team's veterans, comments as he leans over the back of the machine beside mine.

I stop, letting my knees stay curled up into my chest and look at him. "I doubt that."

He chuckles. "So young. So damn cocky. Ah, I miss those days."

I flip him the middle finger and his brother, another guy on our starting offensive line, punches him in the shoulder. "Aw, go easy on him, Noah. He's a newlywed." East grins at me.

I roll my eyes.

"Trouble in paradise already?" Scotch muses.

"I can't imagine why. I mean, Yaeger and his wife have been a sure thing for years, right?" East shrugs.

"Yep." Scotch nods, enthusiastically. "I've heard so much about her, I feel like I know her."

"So many stories I can think of," Easton tacks on.

I groan, both irritated and amused by their dumb display of...whatever the hell this intervention is supposed to be.

"All right, all right." I stand from the machine and grip the bar as my legs feel like jelly. "I get your point."

"When can we meet her?" Scotch asks.

"Yeah," Sims, another guy on the team, hollers out. His eyes are narrowed, and I know that out of everyone on the team, he's the most concerned by my recent nuptials. "Since you just cockblocked yourself for eternity, we should at least know who's behind it."

A blaze of anger burns through me, and I narrow my eyes back at Sims. I don't care for his tone, even though I know he's just pissed that I'm rocking a wedding band, making him the last single guy in our crew.

"Take it easy," East murmurs, his voice quiet but menacing.

Sims swears and stalks out of the locker room.

"He'll come around," Scotch says easily.

I shrug. "There's not much to tell. Vivi and I were…well, we were together in high school."

"High school sweethearts." Scotch clasps his hands, placing them next to his cheek and batting his eyelashes at me.

"Don't ever fucking do that again," his brother growls and I crack a smile.

"Vivi's granddaddy, he's the reason I ever had a shot with hockey. He set me up with all the gear, came to all my games, paid my way for years. Da worked for him and never could have swung the financial or time commitment back then but Mr. Harrison, he was a good man…"

"Was?" Scotch asks.

I nod, scratching my cheek. I suddenly feel uncertain, unsure of absolutely everything. How much information do I share? Will Vivi meet these guys? Does she want to get to know my team? Will she even come to my games and be a part of my…life?

"Look, man, whatever is going on…we don't judge," Scotch offers.

"Seriously. You know how fucked up our relationships started out. Noah knocked Indy up—" East says.

"Easy. I was already stupidly in love with her," Scotch cuts him off.

East shrugs. "I was a fucking mess when Claire and I started out. I made more mistakes than you can imagine. And still, we worked through it. So, if you need to…talk—"

"Holy shit," Scotch interrupts. "You're on some Dr. Phil shit right now."

East flips his brother the bird and I grin, shaking my head. For the briefest flicker of time, I wish I had a brother. A sibling. Someone I could count on to help me navigate this. Of course, Da always has my back. But right now, he's thousands of miles away and I already know how he feels. For some bizarre reason, he thinks Vivi and I are a sure thing. That we make sense even though we sabotaged all the good between us. Yesterday, I told Vivi I was gunning for her heart, and she stared at me like she didn't know whether to believe me.

And truth be told, I don't know how to convince her that I'm worth a damn. How to show her that I can be the man she once trusted.

"She was in a tricky situation," I say lightly.

Automatically, the Scotch brothers' faces change. Their playfulness fades as a seriousness sweeps their expressions, their eyes darkening. Even though Noah's eyes are brown and Easton's are blue, right now, they mirror the same emotions as they stare at me.

"What kind of situation?" East asks, his voice low.

I shake my head, gripping the back of my neck. "Nothing like that. It's just…I swore to her granddaddy I'd look out for her. And then, I saw her face. She needed someone to step in and…"

"You said yes," Scotch surmises.

"Yeah." I look at the two of them. "I stepped in because I couldn't *not* step in. I never stopped loving her and…fuck, I don't have a clue what the fuck I'm doing. I don't know how to…navigate any of this. I'm in so far over my head and…" I cut myself off. Why am I confiding in these guys? Sure, they're my teammates but I'm not this close with them. I'm not *this close* with anyone.

Scotch's expression turns thoughtful. "You need a baby."

"What?" I gasp, wondering for an instant if he knows about Vivi and the miscarriage. No, that makes no goddamn sense. But neither does the way Scotch is grinning like a lunatic.

Easton cuts him a look. "Are you out of your fucking mind? He just got married a…" Easton looks at me.

"A week ago," I supply. A week of awkward silences and feeling like a stranger in my own condo. A week of looking forward to away games and grueling practices so I don't have to share space with Vivi, her sad eyes, and her quiet thoughts. A week until I finally broke down and got the truth from her, only to end up more confused than ever.

"A week ago," Easton repeats.

"No." Scotch shakes his head. "I don't mean have a baby. I mean, you need a baby. Emmaline. The girls need to get together with Genevieve. Indy will bring Emmy. Claire will bring her nosy-ass questions—"

East chuckles in agreement. "Chloe will be all sympathetic and understanding."

"And Abbi will relate to her new move," I add, knowing that Abbi Walsh had one hell of a tough year and a new transition to Boston. If anyone can relate to Vivi, Abbi has the best shot.

"Exactly," Scotch says.

"Okay," I agree, getting on board with this plan of… setting Vivi up on a playdate with a baby and a group of women. Anything to help us move forward. To settle back into some normalcy. To show her that she can build a life here, with me. "I appreciate it, man. I think that would be good for her, to meet some people here, to start making a life. Right now, things are tense, and I want her to feel welcome in Boston."

"Leave it to me," Scotch says seriously.

"Yeah, we'll all sit on each other in your living room," Easton laughs, since Noah and Indy live in a tiny tenement apartment. "Nah, man, Claire and I will have everyone over.

We've got the space and…well, Claire feels like she can ask more questions when we're at our house."

I shake my head but for the first time in a week, I'm grinning. A lightness rolls through my chest, a strange flicker of certainty that something is going to fall into place. Something is going to click and maybe, I'll get a handle on how the hell I can win Vivi back, how we can heal our past and move forward, together.

"This weekend," Easton says.

"We have a game on Saturday," Scotch reminds him.

"Sunday," East says. "We'll do…brunch."

"Brunch?" I quirk an eyebrow. "You got fancy on us, East."

Noah snickers.

East laughs. "It's Claire's favorite."

"Then it's mine too," I say. And I mean it because deep down, I'm grateful that the Scotch brothers have my back.

I'm relieved that the Hawks girls will try with Vivi.

I just need something to give and for the first time since I said I do, I think it might.

"WE'RE GOING TO BRUNCH?" Vivi lifts an eyebrow, looking at me like I just announced I'm running for president.

I smile because the kid I used to be didn't know shit about brunch.

"I still remember teaching you how to eat a formal dinner," Vivi laughs. Whatever she reads in my expression causes her laughter to die and I feel like an ass.

Not because I cared that she was laughing at me, but because I remember that night too. It was the night I made her my girl. The night we made everything that was between us—the long glances, the fumbling kisses, the desirous touches—real. That night I felt like I was flying and now...I can't find my footing with her when being with her used to be more natural than breathing.

"What's wrong?" she whispers.

I tilt my head and sit down on the barstool next to her. She pushes her computer farther down the kitchen island and turns toward me, our bodies squared up and inching forward like a magnet is pulling us. It's always been this way and I'm relieved that even now, with so much unfinished business between us, that tug still exists.

"I'm sorry," I blurt out.

Her eyebrows jump, surprised. "For what?"

"For making you feel like you were alone. This whole time, I was pissed at you for cutting me off. I felt like you pushed me away and, I wasn't there for you."

Her expression softens and I see her again, the woman I first fell in love with. The one I swore I'd never leave. I reach out tentatively and brush my fingers over the back of her hand. She stiffens under my touch but doesn't pull away.

I meet her blue eyes. God, they're filled with so much hesitancy, I hurt staring at them. "Do you think you can ever forgive me?" It's a loaded question, and I'm scared for the answer. Considering our recent conversation, Vivi's wariness, her aloofness toward me makes sense. What if we can never move past what happened?

"I already have, Dec."

"Then what is it? What's holding you back?"

She sighs. "I don't want to get hurt again. I *can't* hurt like that again."

"But Vivi, I would never hurt you. None of that was intentional."

"I know that." She looks at me hard, her eyes fierce. "Of course I know that. But the pain was real, Dec. It took me a long time to feel like myself again, to forgive myself. And since then, it's mostly been just me. I've had to rely on myself for…everything."

"The miscarriage wasn't your fault."

She nods, but tears stain her cheeks. "When I first learned I was pregnant, I was scared. I didn't want to be pregnant; I didn't want to be a single mother. I didn't even want to tell you. And then, when I miscarried, all I could think about was that I wished it. That I caused it."

"But you didn't."

"But I couldn't get past it. God," she sobs, dropping her forehead into her hands and pushing her hair away from her face. "Being with you now, Dec, it brings up so much from the past. Things I thought I was over and now, I'm living through them all over again. And it was hell," she says, her eyes shuddering over. She snatches her hand back and turns back to her computer. "I'm sorry I've been standoffish. I just, I need time. I have some work to finish up."

Frustration fills me at her brush-off, but I don't push her. There's something in her posture, in her tone, that has me holding back. Instead, I stand from my seat and murmur, "Okay."

"But we'll go to brunch," she says as I exit the kitchen.

I stop for a moment and stare at her. Her response is a flicker of hope and right now, I'll take it.

CHAPTER 8
VIVI

His message makes me burst out in laughter and I swipe my phone up off the bathroom counter.

VIVI

Ha!

HENRY

I'm serious. There was a time when you were fun ;)

VIVI

Yeah, a century ago.

HENRY

Things are looking up for you, Viv. Let them.

VIVI

I guess. How's Mac?

HENRY

He sends his love. We're going to the beach this weekend.

VIVI

Have fun.

HENRY

You too. Enjoy brunch.

I scoff and place my phone back down. Staring at my reflection in the mirror, I let out a long exhale. I took time with my appearance today and it shows; I look younger, more approachable than I have in years.

I curled my hair, braiding the top away from my face. My makeup is simple but after years of not wearing much, save for my wedding day, my eyes pop and my skin glows. I've dressed to carefully toe the line between casual and first-impression worthy, pairing simple booties with black jeans and a lightweight, off-the-shoulder sweater.

Gripping the bathroom vanity, I smile. I smile and I see myself, the happy-go-lucky girl underneath the quiet, determined woman. Sometimes, I forget she still exists but right now, I'm happy to see her.

"You got this, Genevieve," I tell myself. "You're going to be fine. You're going to make a friend today." God knows I can use a friend. Except for Declan, I don't know anyone in Boston.

But I'm ready to start trying. As much as I don't understand Granddaddy's reasoning, I'm now married to Declan and running the foundation. I'm embracing my move to Boston, and I'd like it to include a social aspect. I'm ready to mingle, make a few friends, and act like a normal woman in my mid-twenties.

A thrill shoots up my spine—excitement—for Declan to introduce me to his team today. I know that the Hawks have become his pseudo-family since he signed with them over two years ago. I only know this because of the gossip magazines and Mrs. Stevens' insistence that we keep up with his career even though he left us in the dust.

What I don't know is if he wants to introduce me to his team or if he's just following some expectation and protocol. Now that he's married, it would be weird for him not to introduce his wife to anyone in the Hawks franchise.

But when I felt uncertain about going to his game last night, he didn't push it. So, I spent the evening watching it on TV, with a slew of emails to keep me company. It was strange to view Declan the way the world does, through a screen. But it was even weirder to see his hulking frame shadow the door when he arrived home late at night, and I feigned sleep on the couch.

He knocks on the door, two soft raps. "Hey. You almost ready?"

I give myself one last look in the mirror and force my hands to relax their hold on the vanity. Then, I pull open the door. "Yes."

Declan's breath catches when he takes me in. His eyes widen and I hear his sharp inhale as he shuffles back a step. Still, one of his hand remains wrapped around the doorframe.

I hold my breath, biting my bottom lip, waiting for him to say *something*.

"You look..." He pauses, and I die a little inside. "Beautiful. I mean, you're always beautiful, Vivi but..." He trails off again and runs his hand over his mouth. "You look real nice today."

"Thank you," I say softly. Inside, my stomach twists and my heart races at the blatant appreciation in Declan's eyes. His words warm a part of my heart that's been dormant for too long. Eighteen-year-old me rises to the surface and hangs onto his words like sought-after approval. I've been waiting so long to feel pretty again, not just on the outside, but on the inside. And in the span of two breaths, Declan gave me that gift.

I exit the bathroom and Declan moves to let me pass. Grabbing my purse from the kitchen table, I drop my phone inside and slip it onto my shoulder.

"Uh, you might need a coat," he says.

"Huh?" I turn to face him.

His expression is sweet, his eyes kissing the bare skin of my shoulders. "April in Boston is still...fickle. Do you have a jacket?"

"Yeah, of course." I hurry around him to the guest room and retrieve the one coat I have, a vintage, black leather jacket, that keeps looking better with age. I toss it on and re-enter the kitchen.

Now, Declan's eyes nearly bug out of his head. My nerves re-appear, a swarm of bees buzzing around my ears. "What now?"

He shakes his head. "Your mama's coat."

My fingers catch the cuffs and I freeze. "You remember?"

Declan looks at me strange. "Of course, I remember. Jesus, Vivi, I remember the day Mr. Harrison gave it to you."

I smile at the memory, at how the coat dwarfed my petite

frame but how it's warmth still seemed to contain her light. This jacket has seen me through a lot of highs and lows and still, it provides a sliver of comfort and confidence. "Me too. So, I look all right?"

Declan's eyes grow soft, and he holds out a hand. "You look perfect, Vivi."

Grinning at him, I place my hand in his. His touch is familiar, and I cling to that as Declan leads me down to the parking garage and holds the passenger door of his SUV open.

He waits until I'm buckled in before he closes the door. Once he's seated and pulling out of the garage, he glances over at me. "Don't be nervous."

"Am I that obvious?"

"No, I just know you. Relax, Vivi." His hand comes down on my knee and I stare at it, remembering all the times his palm planted on my thigh. It feels right, natural, and I relax under his touch.

After a moment, I place my hand on top of his and he flips his hand over, lacing our fingers together. He pulls into the Boston traffic and grins over at me.

"I'm happy you're here. In Boston."

"Me too."

"At first, I didn't know if you'd want to stay in Tennessee. I didn't know if we'd even try to make our marriage real," he admits, his expression curious.

"I didn't either. I don't know what we're doing but it feels…"

"What?"

"Right," I say, smiling at him.

Dec smiles back and it hits me full on. "Feels right for me too, babe."

I turn to look out the window and we settle into a comfortable silence. Now that the secret is out in the open,

I'm not worrying about it all the time. For the first time since our wedding day, I relax and vow to enjoy this time with Declan.

To make an effort with his team and have fun at brunch.

SHE'S PRETTY.

That's my first thought of Claire Merrick, the blonde-haired, blue-eyed, enthusiastic woman who pulls open the door to the brownstone.

"You're here! Congratulations!" she announces, like she's known me for years. Then, her arms dart out and she pulls me into a hug that has me chuckling because of how unexpected it is. "We look alike," she decides when she pulls away.

I shake my head, smiling at her. I have no idea what to make of Claire other than that in the two seconds I've known her, I like her. I've also not met anyone like her before.

"Claire." A hulking man with the bluest eyes I've ever seen appears behind her. "Take it easy, yeah?"

Claire scoffs and rolls her eyes, stepping forward to kiss Declan's cheek. "You did good, Yaeger."

Declan chuckles and runs his hand through his curls, embarrassed. "Thanks for having us."

"Anytime man, you know that," the guy says, turning to me and sticking out a hand. "I'm Easton."

"Genevieve," I say, shaking his hand. "It's nice to meet you."

"Oh God, I'm swooning," Claire says, bouncing up onto her toes. "Keep talking."

"Jesus," Easton mutters. "Come on, let me take your coat."

He pulls me past the foyer as Claire's laughter rings out behind him.

I glance over my shoulder at Declan, and he gives me a reassuring nod before dropping his head to better hear whatever Claire is whispering.

"Don't be nervous," Easton says, and I swing my gaze to his, surprised he can tell. "I know it's a lot. All these people, Declan's life with hockey, Boston. But your man is a good guy, and we all care about him. I know he really cares about you…" My eyebrows fly up and Easton snorts. "We're all happy you're here. If you need anything"—he opens an arm to where a table of laughing, coffee and mimosa-drinking women sit, one of them with a baby in her arms—"these are the women to ask. Where to shop, if you need a plumber or a painter, a dinner reservation, or a car rental, they have all the answers."

I smile warmly, relieved that I feel comfortable when I was certain this entire day would be awkward. I shrug out of Mama's jacket and Easton takes it as a few of the women stand.

"Hi! Good to meet you, Genevieve. I'm Indy." The woman with the baby bounces the sweet girl in her arms. "And this is Emmaline."

"Hi." I wave.

"I'm Chloe!" A fellow blonde shifts to pour a mimosa and hands it to me.

"Abbi." A woman waves, clinking her glass against mine.

"Hey, I'm Bella," a sweet-looking woman says, coming up beside me. She places a plate of doughnuts in the center of the table. "I got the goods."

"Sprinkles!" Chloe cheers, scooping up a doughnut.

"Better grab one if you want to eat at all," Abbi jokes as Bella points to an empty chair and I drop into it.

"Don't listen to her," Claire says, entering the space and

sitting beside me. "I have a whole other box hidden from the guys."

At that, the entire table erupts in laughter, and I find myself smiling with them. They're easygoing and inclusive and as I turn to glance at Declan over my shoulder, I realize that he's introducing me to his family here in the U.S. And suddenly, I want nothing more than to belong.

CHAPTER 9
DECLAN

"How's it going?" Austin asks, passing me a beer.

"Not bad." I pop the top and clink it against his before taking a sip. "Thanks."

He nods. "Look, man, I know I was harsh last week with Coach and—"

"No," I cut him off, lifting my beer. "I shouldn't have walked away from the team like that."

"Yeah. But you're married…"

"I'm married," I agree, glancing at Vivi. She's sitting with the Hawks women, a serene smile on her lips and an expression of wonder on her face.

"They're overwhelming the hell out of her," Austin laughs.

I chuckle with him but as I watch Genevieve, I don't think she minds. For the first time since we've reconnected, she looks…relaxed. At ease. The tension that resides in her shoulders has receded and her expression is smooth. "She's fine."

"How's married life?" Scotch asks, standing next to Austin.

I take a long pull of my beer and the guys laugh.

"It's new," I say after a moment. "Things between us are…"

"Complicated," Scotch supplies.

"Very," I agree. But I can't tear my eyes away from Vivi when I say it. Things between us are all over the place. I married her because I couldn't *not* marry her; she married me because she wanted to run the foundation. That's complicated.

But learning about the baby? Understanding all the miscommunications and assumptions we made years ago, the hurt we both caused each other, the guilt we both feel? That's a hell of a lot more than complicated. Our relationship is straight up convoluted, a maze of messy feelings and uncertainties. A labyrinth of faded dreams and broken trust we're trying to muddle through, to restore.

At least, I am. But what about her?

Standing here now and watching Genevieve interact with my friends' women, it fills me with a strange nostalgia. A sadness I wish I could chase away. I realize how many years we missed, how many moments we should have shared and didn't.

Vivi was right to put distance between us. I don't know her anymore. Not her body, not her thoughts, and certainly not her heart. But I want to. If I didn't, her aloofness wouldn't bother me as much as it does. I want to know my wife the way I used to. I want to win her back.

James pulls Noah and Austin into a conversation about next week's game in Atlanta and I inch closer to the table where the women have stolen all the good food, leaving us with omelets and turkey bacon.

"The Harrison Foundation has many philanthropic programs across the country. I'd like to expand our initiatives aimed at female empowerment. While I didn't think it would be in Boston, I'm happy to be here to learn about the community's needs and how the Harrison Foundation can meet them," Vivi explains to Abbi.

"What are some of the programs?" Abbi asks and I tip my head, wanting to know more about the foundation, the legacy Vivi needed to protect.

"Breast cancer awareness and children's literacy were the two causes most dear to my granddaddy. Mostly because my grandmother started those programs before she passed. But Granddaddy also contributed to the Red Cross, to several schools designed for female education in developing countries, and initiatives to end whaling. He had his fingers in a million different things but only the things he felt passionate about. I think that was one of the greatest lessons he ever shared with me. To do something that fills you up on the inside, not just your pockets. Passion is important."

"Absolutely," Abbi agrees, taking a sip of her mimosa. "I love working in Youth Outreach because sports and kids combine two of the things I care most about."

"That's awesome," Vivi says, leaning back in her seat.

"Have you always wanted to expand the foundation's work with women?" Abbi asks.

I shift closer, desperate to learn more about Vivi. At home, she's amiable but not engaging. Right now, she's connecting with Abbi and I don't want to miss out on glimpsing the parts of her I remember.

"Absolutely. Female empowerment, resources for women after abuse, rape, loss. I'd like to start a shelter, a whole series of shelters, a program that lends support to women when they find themselves in impossible situations." The more Genevieve speaks, the more the other girls at the table tune in. Silence begins to descend on the space, but she doesn't notice and I'm glad, because she keeps talking. "I'd love to create something that offers a physical space women can go, with the support systems in place to help them cope, and financial mechanisms that can provide long-term solutions. Of course, many of these shelters already exist, so I'd need to identify areas where more support is necessary. Too many women, especially with children, don't have the means to leave bad situations." She shakes her head, her eyes flashing with indignation. For a moment, she looks like she did in high school, taking on the school board to advocate for the inclusion of a female football player on an all-male team. Vivi's always had a stake in the battle against injustice and I love that she didn't lose that fire, that passion, to help others. "I for sure want to focus on women. If I could ever be so fortunate as to have a legacy…it'd be that."

Abbi smiles at her before Claire starts clapping.

Vivi grins, but ducks her head in embarrassment.

Claire whistles. "Sign me up, Genevieve Yaeger. That's the smartest thing I've heard any of us say and my cousin Indy's a professor."

Genevieve Yaeger. I like the sound of that.

Vivi turns even redder and a thread of worry snakes through my chest, pulling taut, as I wait for her to tell the girls that she didn't change her name. Or that she's not really a Yaeger. But she surprises me by chuckling with the girls and looking at Indy. "Can I tap into your network?"

"Anytime, girl. I'd love to work on the vision you're building," Indy answers easily.

"Once you get started, let me know. We can always run a piece in the paper," Chloe offers. I forgot she's a journalist.

My girl beams. Her entire face transforms and it's like a punch to the gut. Because I know that smile, I've seen it every damn day, mostly in my dreams, since she first turned it on me when I was thirteen.

And I miss it. I miss her.

SINCE RETURNING FROM BRUNCH, Vivi has kept to herself, going straight to her room, the sound of her fingers clacking against the keyboard the only thing to keep me company.

Instead of hitting the gym or getting in a run, I've paced in the damn living room, wondering what the hell has become of my life.

Genevieve Rae used to be as familiar to me as the glide of ice beneath my skates, as the Nashville skyline, as the feeling of *not* fitting in. In a land of cowboy boots and country music, my hockey-loving, Vans-sporting ass didn't fit in. But Vivi made me a home. A safe place that existed between her arms.

And now, I don't know how to connect with her. Sure, she's polite, friendly even. But that natural charisma, the way we used to know what the other person was thinking, doesn't exist anymore. And I want it back. When I can't take it anymore, I rap on her doorframe. Only to be met with her wide blue eyes and a perfect little Cupid's bow of a mouth. A mouth I used to kiss whenever I wanted.

"You hungry?"

"Sure," she says slowly, angling her head to study me. She's looking at me like she doesn't understand why I'd ask her to kick it, to do anything, and that bothers me too.

Doesn't she remember the connection we once had? Doesn't she care that we're now freaking married?

She glances down at her laptop screen before closing it. Then she takes a deep breath and squares her shoulders. Something pulls in my chest. Something uncomfortable and tight. Shame fills my stomach and I shuffle a step closer to her.

"Vivi, look," I breathe out, leaning against her desk. "I know things are complicated between us."

"That's an understatement."

I smirk and her expression softens.

"We used to be friends," I remind her. "More than that."

She nods and stands from her desk chair. "Give me a few minutes to freshen up?"

"Sure." I step back. "What are you in the mood for?"

"Surprise me." Her tone is dry but playfulness sparks in her eyes.

"I know a place." I head into my room. Pulling on a sweater and jeans, I slip into Chelsea boots. I never truly fit in in Tennessee but the remnants of the style, boots and belts, kind of stuck with me after I moved away.

I head back into the living room, staring at Vivi's door, until it swings open, and she emerges. My breath catches in my throat, and I look away. That's the thing with Vivi. She's so stunning, so bright and good, that sometimes, looking at her hurts. It's like trying to stare at the sun.

"Ready?"

"Yep." I swipe up my keys and wallet and lead her down to the parking garage.

Once we settle in, I point the SUV toward the West End. "Still like Mexican?"

She grins. "You know it's my favorite."

"You'll love this place. It's Mexican…fusion."

"Fusion?" She quirks an eyebrow. "Y'all are fancy up here in Boston."

I chuckle. "There's sushi nachos." I glance over and take in the wrinkle in her nose. "Nope, don't knock 'em 'til you've tried 'em. They were so popular, the owners added sushi fajitas to the menu."

Vivi snorts and holds up a hand. "All right, I'll reserve judgement till after we eat. You come here often?"

I pull into a parking space a few buildings down from Noah and Indy's apartment, a close walk to the restaurant.

"Some of the guys on the team introduced me to it. It's become a favorite over the past year." I point at Scotch's place. "Noah and Indy live there."

Her eyes widen. "In that building?"

I laugh. "Yeah. It's a tenement apartment."

"I'm surprised they wouldn't want something…newer."

"Or bigger," I agree. "Especially now with the baby. But Indy likes the history and Scotch likes whatever Indy does so…"

A sad sweetness rolls over Vivi's expression. "I get that. I like them." She glances at me. "All of your friends. The girls. I had no idea what to expect, what they would be like, but they're awesome."

"Yeah," I agree, my hand planting on her thigh. "They liked you too."

She wrinkles her nose. "How could you tell?"

"I just could. What's not to like, anyway?"

She tips her head back and laughs. The sound is pure music and I revel in it. Love that I made her laugh at all.

"Y'all clicked, especially you and Abbi. But all of the girls would jump in to help you with the foundation's work."

She smirks at me. "I haven't heard you say *y'all* once since I've seen you and now you're tossing it around like it's normal."

I tip my head back into the headrest. "Ah, yeah. Kind of lost my accent." I roll my head to look at her. "But I missed yours, Vivi."

She laughs and shakes her head, not believing me. Oh, but I have. I've missed her and her laughter and her spirit.

"I miss having girlfriends," she admits. "I haven't had any since high school and we all lost touch afterwards. Since then, I haven't connected with anyone I trust. Not the way I trust Henry."

Damn, it still hurts something fierce hearing her say it. That Henry's her constant, the guy who got her through her toughest days. But I'm still happy she had him, that she had someone she could count on, since it sure as hell wasn't me.

I guess it bothers me because Henry was always on the periphery of our little trio but now…I am. And after so many years away, why wouldn't I be? But when you leave a place, even though your world grows and your horizon shifts, even though you meet new people and have new experiences, you never think your home place changes too. I guess in some ways, the ways that matter, it alters too much. And if you try to go home, you're the one trying to fit back in.

"The team, they're like my family here, Genevieve. They know we're married. They know it all happened suddenly. But they won't pump you for information. They won't put you on blast. You can make your own friendships with them."

The corner of her mouth ticks up. "I'd like that."

"And I heard you talking to the girls today too. About the foundation and your work. I think it's amazing," I say truthfully. "It's so you."

She smiles.

"Anything I can help with—"

"Seriously?" she cuts me off.

"Seriously."

"Thanks, Dec."

I nod. "I'm here for you, Vivi. I know this is a big transition. I know things are confusing and kind of weird. But I don't want to keep living in the condo with all this awkwardness between us."

"Me neither. I missed you," she says quietly, like it's a confession. "More than you'll ever know."

At the sadness in her voice, I lean forward. I place my hand over hers, relieved when she doesn't pull away.

"We're in this together now. Whatever the hell this is, it's ours. There's no reason it can't be good."

"Okay." She shoots me a smile.

"Okay." I smile back, feeling like we've come to some type of understanding.

We exit the car and I point in the direction of the restaurant. As we head toward it, I can't help but feel like I'm on a first date. A second chance first date where the future seems full of possibilities. Full of hope again.

CHAPTER 10
VIVI

"We'll take the sushi nachos to start," Dec orders.

"And to drink?" our server, Shell, asks.

Declan glances at me, waiting.

I narrow my eyes but I'm grinning. This is it, the moment I take a step forward with him or retreat into myself. But over the past two weeks, Declan has consistently showed up for me. He married me, for crying out loud. And since learning the truth about *that* summer, he's done nothing but try to connect with me, to make me feel at home, to bring me into his life and into our marriage.

At the hopeful look in his eyes, the expectation in his face, I finally give in. "Two margaritas on the rocks. Patron. Extra salt." And those words are my undoing. Those are the words that break the dam on all the emotions I've been holding back from him.

"Got it." Shell scurries away.

Declan flashes me the biggest smile I've ever seen before tipping his head back and laughing. The sound is deep and sexy, causing the hairs on my arms to stand. His shoulders roll forward and I can't tear my eyes away from checking him out. The way his muscles move, the bulge of his biceps, the bob of his Adam's apple. I gulp.

Living down the hall from him, trying to keep distance between us, has been hell. Especially because of how caring he's been. His sincerity knows no bounds and now, mixed with his undeniable hotness, well, my mouth dries. It's like my ordering our drinks, our old go-to, was the first slide down a slippery slope. Because now, I have no defense against the attraction blazing to life inside of me. If only he knew that every night, I go to sleep thinking of him, just down the hallway, and wishing for his touch.

Declan's eyes are warm with laughter and something else. Relief. "You remember?"

I grin, amused and…happy. "The first night you got me drunk, Declan Yaeger? I puked behind Granddaddy's mulberry trees and—"

"Da cleaned it up the next morning," he finishes, grinning hard. "He was furious."

I laugh. "You held my hair back."

"I slept in your bed, petrified you were going to throw up in your sleep."

I groan at the memory, at the awful hangover that followed. "I thought I was going to die."

"You? When I wasn't worried about your vomiting, I was petrified Mr. Harrison was going to burst through the door with his shotgun and shoot me."

A bubble of laughter springs forth, surprising us both. But I tip my head in agreement. "He would have. Granddaddy was always worried about my virtue."

"He didn't have to worry with me. I was a fumbling fool when it came to you."

"I did have to make all the first moves," I agree, sticking my tongue out at him.

Declan's cheeks blaze red, and I laugh. He holds up a

hand. "In my defense, I was trying to be a good guy. I didn't want to pressure you."

"You made us wait two years to have sex," I remind him.

"We were sixteen," he retorts.

"Exactly."

Declan groans and shakes his head but we're both biting back our smiles.

"This is nice," I tell him.

He dips his head. "I know. I missed you, Vivi."

"Me too, Dec."

Shell drops off our drinks and we order dinner.

Declan raises his glass in my direction. "To new beginnings."

"To us," I say, meaning it, as I clink my glass against his.

Declan's eyes hold mine, liquid heat, as he takes a sip of his margarita. "Does this mean you're going to give me a shot?"

"Us," I clarify. "I want to give us a chance. We both made mistakes, we both could have done better. And if this is going to work, we both need to try."

Declan's eyes are solemn as they hold mine. "You're right. I won't let you down again, Vivi."

"And I'll be more…honest. Forthcoming," I promise.

"Good," he says seriously before his expression turns playful. "And whenever you're ready to move into the master bedroom—"

I groan, but I'm grinning. If only he knew how badly I want *that* part to happen. "You'll be the first to know."

"I'd hope so, Genevieve."

"Or maybe I'll make you wait as long as you kept me waiting," I say coyly.

Declan's mouth drops open. "Two years?"

At the despair in his tone, I crack up and he joins in. In fact, by the time our entrees arrive, we've fallen back into our old selves. Playful, flirty, and so damn into each other that the rest of the restaurant falls away.

Over the course of the evening, I find myself sharing more about the foundation, about the past seven years, about myself with Declan. He listens intently, asking questions and making jokes. He shares his hopes for the season, his disbelief about starting for the Hawks this year, his dreams for the future.

Over enchiladas and fajitas, we become reacquainted with each other. The candle between us burns lower and the margaritas flow like water. By the time we're back home, with the condo door closed behind us, I feel like myself again.

I turn and gaze up at Declan, my hands on his hips to steady myself. His eyes are hooded, colored with desire. My heart rate ticks up, eager to see how this plays out. Will he kiss me? Or will I have to make the first move, the same way I did when I was twelve?

As if reading my thoughts, Declan's lips twitch. "You gotta give me a chance, babe."

"For what?" I tilt my head.

"To step up for you," he says, his hands darting out. His fingers loop through my belt buckles and he tugs me closer until our legs collide. "To show up for you." His voice drops several octaves.

My breathing grows heavy as we stare into each other's eyes. The space between us evaporates as we lean toward each other, captivated by the magnetic pull that still exists between us.

"I'm going to kiss you now, Genevieve," Dec whispers right before his mouth closes over mine.

My eyes flutter closed, and I lose myself, wholeheartedly, in his kiss. In his touch. In the feel of his lips moving over mine. I tip my face up and one of Declan's hands finds my cheek, angling my head as he kisses me harder.

I part my lips, half on a gasp and half in need for more.

My hands grip his sides, my breasts press into his abdomen, and I revel in his kiss the same way I did when I was a teenager. He kisses me with intention and promise, with apology and need, with all the words he hasn't said and all the things I needed to hear.

When he pulls back, I'm panting.

Declan presses his forehead against mine. "Vivi."

I force my eyes open.

"That's all we're doing tonight."

Huh? I pull back to glare at him.

He winks, the dimple in his cheek popping.

I laugh and pinch his side.

He grabs my hand and holds my fingers tight.

"You're such a tease," I accuse him, mainly because it's bullshit and if one of us has been giving mixed signals, it's been me.

But Dec takes it in stride and laughs with me. "Gotta play my cards right this time," he says, kissing the top of my head. "I won't lose you again."

I sink into his warmth and let him lead me to the living room, where we watch TV and joke around, much like we did in high school, until I fall asleep. At some point, I feel Declan slip his arms around me and cradle me against his chest.

"But I still want you in my bed," he murmurs as he tucks me in, pulling his grey duvet over my shoulders. Then, he kisses my nose, I smile, and sleep claims me.

CHAPTER 11

DECLAN

HENRY

Tell me he at least kissed you.

I chuckle, and turn Vivi's cell phone facedown so I'm not tempted to read her messages. Even though they're about me. I grin, a little too happy that she and Henry talk about me. Does Henry want us to get back together?

Maybe the guy I was jealous over is really on my side. Maybe I was too quick to judge their relationship.

The ring of Vivi's cell interrupts my thoughts and I stare at it, debating. I'm not proud of it, but my curiosity wins, and I answer her phone.

"Henry."

A pause. "Declan? Why're you answering Viv's phone. Is she okay? Tell me you guys finally got out of your own damn way and she's just sleeping off her orgasmic bliss."

Huh? I burst out in laughter. "What the hell are you talking about, man?"

"Damn. Y'all still haven't done it?"

"Henry, it's not like that between me and Vivi," I fib, not wanting to kiss and tell.

"Yeah fucking right. Y'all know it should be."

I clear my throat, both uncomfortable and amused by the turn this conversation has taken. "Well, *I* know that but Vivi…" I trail off. Last night, she definitely would have slept with me. But I don't just want her body. I want all of her. Heart and soul and thoughts. Everything she holds back.

Henry laughs. "She still giving you a hard time, making you work for it?"

"That's one way to say it."

His laughter grows. "God, I love that girl."

Me too. I love her so damn much, I don't know how I existed this long without her. But I don't say that. I just wait for Henry to keep talking, to give me something to work with. Since he's her best friend and all.

Henry sighs, "You gotta be patient, man. Win back her trust. After y'all broke up…"

"I know."

"You know what?" he asks cryptically, and I grin because Vivi was right, Henry is a true friend.

"I know about the baby. The…miscarriage."

He blows out an exhale. "Finally. I'm glad she told you."

"So am I. I had no idea. If I knew, you know I'd have come back."

"I know," Henry agrees. "And you did come back, remember? She just wouldn't see you."

"Yeah," I scoff. "You know, I saw you guys."

"What?"

"I came home my sophomore year of college. I saw you and Vivi training, with boxing gloves. She was laughing and I thought…"

"That we were together," he finishes.

"Yes."

"You're a fucking idiot."

I laugh.

"Viv's only ever had eyes for you, Declan. I used to have to push her to go out on dates—"

I frown. Of course, Vivi dated but…I don't really want to hear about.

"And the whole time, she compared the guy to you."

That makes me smile. "She date a lot?"

Henry chuckles. "No way am I going there, man. Just, open your eyes, Declan. You're getting a second chance. Use it."

His words hit me hard. Because he's right. A second chance, a fresh start. An opportunity to prove to Vivi that I'm the guy she once believed me to be. I was fooling myself if I ever thought my marriage to Vivi was motivated by a promise to Mr. Harrison. It was a convenient excuse, but never the reason.

The truth is, I never stopped loving her. It's the same reason I stayed away for so damn long. I was hurt and angry because… I fucking love her.

I chuckle, shaking my head at myself. No wonder all the other women never mattered, never even made an impression. Genevieve Rae Kelley has always been my only and marrying her, even under these pretenses, is a gift. One I won't waste.

"I'm trying, man. I hate that I didn't fight harder for her back then." I lean back against the kitchen countertop. "For us."

"Look, Viv's my best friend and what she went through that summer was hell. But Declan, y'all were eighteen, broken up, and about to go off to college. You didn't act differently than any other eighteen-year-old kid with a broken heart in a foreign country. One where you were of legal drinking age."

His words loosen some of the knots in my chest. "I appreciate that man, but me and Vivi, I should have known it was more than the breakup. I should have done something."

"Ugh," he mutters. "You both are annoying. So damn self-sacrificing. Listen to me, you're still doing it, you're standing in y'all's way. Be there for her now, show her she can trust you, and give her time to accept it. You of all people know how stubborn she is."

"Yeah," I say, my tone filled with pride. Vivi's stubbornness is part of the reason why she's so successful, why she's able to help as many people as she has. "That's good advice. Thanks, Henry."

"That's what I'm here for."

"What are you doing this weekend?" I ask, making small talk.

He laughs, because he knows I probably don't give a shit, but I'm minding my manners. I hear a male voice in the background and Henry laughs harder. "Heading to the beach."

"You get a roommate?" As far as I know, from Vivi, Henry lives alone.

His laughter fades. "Kind of."

I glance at the phone, frowning. What kind of answer is that?

"Um, okay," I say slowly.

Henry snorts. "Take care of our girl, Declan. It was good talking to you."

"Yeah, you too."

"I hope you guys find what you used to have."

"I hope so too. Maybe the next time we're back in Nashville, we can grab a beer," I toss out, feeling grateful toward my old friend when a few weeks ago, I wanted to knock him out.

"We'll see, Yaeger. First, make our girl fall for you again. Then, we can see about a beer."

"Deal. Have fun at the beach."

"Later."

I end the call and place Vivi's phone down.

A renewed energy fills my veins as I walk back to my bedroom. Last night, Vivi slept in my arms, and it was the best sleep I had in years. I loved waking up to her face, the scent of her shampoo this morning. I peer inside the room at her sleeping body, the rise and fall of her chest. My girl deserves so much more than she ever got. I need to prove to her that she can trust me. That I'm here for her.

That I'm not going anywhere.

"I GOT YOU SOMETHING," I tell her a week later, dropping my practice bag on the floor.

She arches her eyebrows, glancing up from her laptop.

I pass her a bag and she shoots me a smirk before peering inside. "A jersey?"

"Expecting a spa appointment?"

She laughs. "No, I just, does this mean you want me to come to a game?"

"I'd like you to come to more than one," I say truthfully. *I want you to come to the whole damn season. To sit in the box with the wives and the girlfriends and make friends. To laugh and joke and chat again, the way you used to.*

The past week has been a turning point for Vivi and me. Gone is the stilted silence and beats of awkwardness. Instead, everything is infused with an awareness now. There's a hum that exists between us, one filled with sexual tension and hesitancy. I want to erase the hesitancy, but I won't take Vivi until I know she's giving me more than just the night.

But, we're getting there. Because this past week has also seen more honest conversations and silly horsing around than I've had in years.

"Can I come to the game on Saturday? Against Chicago?" she asks.

"Look at you, knowing our schedule."

She grins.

"Yeah, I'd love that. You cool sitting with the other girls, in the family box?" I drop into the chair next to her at the kitchen table.

She closes the top of her laptop and slides it away, giving me her full attention. It feels good, to have her turn those baby blues my way and really look at me.

"Will Indy and Claire be there?"

"Abbi and Chloe too. Probably Bella if she decides to bring the twins."

"Okay. Yeah, then I'll be good to go."

"Great." I stand from my chair, brushing a kiss over her hair as I make my way into the kitchen. I pour two glasses of water, aware of her gaze on my back. While our interactions have thawed and are now definitely friendly, I've been careful not to do anything more than kiss her.

But damn if it's not hard when her hair smells like tangerines and her mouth taunts me with its perfect bow.

I place a water in front of her. "What are you working on?"

She slides her laptop back over and opens it. The screen illuminates a document, showcasing several real estate options, as well as a prospectus of sorts.

"Real estate?" My eyebrows lift and I turn toward her.

She nods, the corner of her mouth pulling upwards. "I'm going to start my first shelter here, in Boston. I told you that the first women's shelter in the country was started here, right?"

I nod. "In the seventies."

"In 1974. Rosie's Place. Can you believe it took until the seventies until women had a resource like that?"

"No," I say, thickly. "I can't."

"I know. I'm going to meet with one of the directors at another shelter to learn more about programs in Boston. I'd like to either support an existing mission or plug a hole that the community needs but currently doesn't have access to."

"What kind of hole?"

She tucks her legs underneath her and turns into me, her eyes sparking with that dazzle I love so much. "You know, job training, education resources, or maybe something more urgent, with a food shelter component. I was doing this type of research and planning in Nashville, but Boston is different. I want to learn about the needs of this community before I go dreaming up an idea that may not be the most beneficial."

I stare at her, mesmerized because 1. She's right. And 2. Isn't that beautiful? That my selfless girl is still putting others first. "I'm in awe of you."

She blushes, a rosy glow flaring over her cheekbones. Dropping her head she murmurs, "It's nothing yet."

"Don't say that. It's already something. And it's a great something. I'm proud of you, Vivi."

At my tone, she looks up and ducks her head the tiniest bit. "Thank you."

"So, how can I help?"

"Actually, would you come with me? I'm meeting the realtor to see some properties and I'd love a second opinion."

I grin at the olive branch she's extending. She's including me in her work, in her dream. She values my opinion. It feels good to have her place some trust in me again.

It's such a simple moment and yet, it shifts everything. It's the moment when I know, down to my bones, that I want to build the most beautiful future with this woman. That I can't, won't lose her at the end of this year. That I'll do everything in my power to make her *want* to stay.

I grip her chin, my thumb pressing into its center as I lift her face to meet mine. "I'd love to. Just let me know the day and time. I'll be there."

A slow smile stretches across her face, until she's luminous, lighting up the room with all that beauty and light she's kept locked up for God knows how long.

"Thanks, Dec."

"Don't thank me, babe. Just let me in."

"I'm trying," she murmurs, holding my eyes when I figured she'd look away.

I lean the slightest bit closer. Her eyes flare but she doesn't pull back. "You're doing great, Vivi. Really, really great."

"I've never been to anything like this!" I shout to Claire, who's dancing in the seat next to mine.

"Ooh, I love this for you!" she squeals, throwing her arms up in the air as the Boston Hawks are introduced.

As the players take the ice, Abbi lets loose with cat calls that Chloe echoes. While a few people nearby shoot looks in our direction, the box filled with family members is too busy having a good time to notice.

I laugh and hide my face in my hands. Anticipation for the game, for tonight, rolls through me. It's been ages since I've felt like this, giddy and rowdy and excited for whatever unfolds.

Tonight feels different. With these women by my side and Declan skating onto the ice, I feel like I belong. I feel like I'm part of the BHH family and Declan is truly my husband, not just in name. When his name is announced, I holler out cheers.

"Thatta girl." Claire bumps her hip next to mine.

Even though the arena is packed and there is no way Declan heard me, his eyes meet mine when I call out his name. He flashes me the most breathtaking smile and I can't help but grin back, smiling so hard my cheeks hurt.

"Damn, you guys are cute," Chloe says. "How's married life?"

"Not nearly as bad as I thought," I blurt out, honest.

The girls look surprised for a beat before they erupt into laughter. I laugh with them, relaxing fully into the social circle I feel blessed to be included in.

"Well…" Indy says slowly, sidling up to the grouping of chairs we're occupying. "You may ask me that soon, too." She holds up her left hand where a gorgeous diamond engagement ring sparkles.

"Oh my God!" Claire lunges for her cousin, hugging her hard. "How the hell did you not tell me?"

"Congratulations!" I exclaim.

"Show us the ring," Abbi demands, pulling Indy into a chair with Claire still attached to her. Claire perches in Indy's lap, taking her hand and jutting it out for all of us to ooh and ahh over.

But truly, the three-carat oval cut set in a platinum band is both elegant and beautiful.

"It just happened," Indy gushes, her happiness radiating around her like an aura. I inch closer, hoping some of it rubs off on me.

"Tonight?" Claire's head whips toward Indy's.

Indy nods. "I wasn't even going to come tonight because Emmaline's been so fussy. And then, right before Noah left for the arena, Emmy spit up down the front of my shirt and I was feeling just so…crappy. You know? I was overwhelmed and frustrated about missing the game and," she laughs, shaking her head, "I opened my eyes and there's Noah, down on one knee."

"What?" Chloe shrieks.

"He's losing his touch," Claire remarks, but her eyes are dancing and I know she's joking.

"Oh, he had a whole plan but he said he didn't want to spend one more second without his ring on my finger. That even covered in Emmy's spit up I'm more beautiful than any woman he's ever known. And that there's no place he feels more at home than in our tiny, cramped kitchen." Tears spring into Indy's eyes and I feel my throat tighten at the emotion she shares so easily.

It's a gift, to be that honest and open with your feelings. Confident enough in yourself, and your surroundings, to feel freely. I used to have that with Declan and now…we're getting there again.

"I take it back. He's the best," Claire laughs, kissing Indy's temple. "I'm so happy for you, Indy."

"Me too!" Abbi gushes. "That story was—"

"The freaking sweetest," Bella announces, sitting down next to me. "I just caught the end of that proposal and…" She trails off, wiping tears from the corners of her eyes. "Congratulations, my friend. I—Mason, don't stick that up your nose," she calls out to James's son, off her seat and headed toward the eight-year-old.

Indy looks at me, her expression softening. "Will you help me plan my wedding?"

"What?" I gasp, wondering if she's talking to me.

Indy shrugs. "You're my only friend in Boston who recently married. I have no idea where to start, what to begin with. If you don't mind weighing in, since you just planned your wedding, I'd appreciate it."

"I, um, of course," I say, taken aback by her request. And humbled by her friendship. "I'd love to," I say more firmly. No one needs to know that I planned a wedding to Henry, not Declan. But still, knowing it was the only wedding I'd ever have, I planned most of it true to my heart. The tiny flickering lights in the garden, the magnolias in church, the dress of my dreams. All of it was sincere and then, I glance toward the ice, my gaze zeroing in on number four, I married the man of my dreams too.

I may not have admitted it then. But now, it's only been a little over a month, and I feel more like my old self, my true self, than I have in years.

Our conversation stays centered on wedding chatter. In the past, I would have held back but with these girls, I find myself weighing in on flower arrangements and the best season to hold a wedding. I find myself laughing and nodding and ordering another cocktail.

"We're going to win this game," Claire says knowingly. "Then, we're going to Taps to celebrate!" She glances at Indy.

Indy nods. "Yes, my mom has Emmy for the night."

"Woohoo!" Abbi dances in her chair, her arms lifted over her head and crossed at the wrist like she's in the club. "Gotta get my man liquored up so we can go home and—"

"No details." Chloe shields her eyes instead of her ears which makes me laugh. "And we all know Panda doesn't need an ounce of liquor to make things hot for ya."

I spit out my drink, choking on the margarita.

Claire smacks my back. "You're scaring her." She points at Abbi.

"You're killing me," I agree but for an entirely different reason. "I haven't, I've never had friends before who are so, so—"

"Beautiful," Claire says seriously.

Chloe rolls her eyes. "Forward?"

"Loud," Indy guesses.

"Fun!" Abbi cheers.

"Honest," Bella says, sitting back down and I point to her.

"I was going to go with honest," I admit.

The girls laugh. "Well, welcome to the group, Vivi," Claire says, using Declan's name for me. For years I was Genevieve or Viv. Only Declan calls me Vivi and yet...I like that his people do too.

I lift my glass and tell them truthfully. "I'm happy to be here."

"We're happy to have you." Chloe clinks her glass against mine.

Then a cheer rings through the arena, the energy pulsing as the crowd starts to do The Wave.

"Oh brother," Claire mutters.

"Come on," Indy laughs, pulling her up.

We all join in, acting silly and laughing way too hard, until the Hawks win 5-3. Then, the girls pull me toward the hallway outside the locker room to wait for the guys.

My heart races as a burst of nerves zips through my limbs. This feels different. While Declan and I have fallen into some kind of a relationship over the past week, it hasn't progressed to more than sweet kisses. But right now, tonight, I feel like it finally could.

I'm here as his wife. I've spent the night laughing with his friends.

He pushes through the door, nodding and smiling at his teammates' families as he passes them. But then his eyes slam into mine and he strides toward me, all purposeful and possessive.

"Damn," Abbi mutters.

"Hell yeah," Chloe agrees.

I gape at him, getting lost in the heat in his eyes. He's clean shaven, his hair still damp from a shower. His sweater is black and hugs his muscles deliciously. His eyes narrow as he steps up to me and I shuffle back, my spine meeting the wall.

"Nice game," I mutter.

Abbi laughs.

Declan grins. "Nice, huh? You watch it?"

I bite my bottom lip and slowly shake my head because truth be told, I pretty much missed the whole thing, having way too much fun with the girls.

My answer pleases Declan though because he smirks and plants one hand flat against the wall beside my head. My friends have disappeared, but it wouldn't matter because right now, I only have eyes for Declan.

He peers down at me, his eyes a complicated swirl of emotions. They darken and his nostrils flare. His lips part and he drops his head the tiniest bit, a hopeful request in his eyes.

But I know what he wants. He wants to claim me, in front of his team, in front of the world. He wants me to be his *wife*.

I straighten to my full height and lift my chin, flashing him a dare.

A small chuckle falls from his lips and then, he drops his head and kisses me like I'm his oxygen, like he can't survive without me.

The meeting of our lips rips me back to the past and catapults me into the future. Chills dance down my spine and heat fans in the pit of my stomach. I gasp and Declan uses my surprise to slip his tongue inside my mouth. My eyes close, my hands find purchase on his shoulders, and I melt into him, desirous, ravenous, and so damn happy.

TAPS ISN'T AT ALL like I expected. As the big, brawny hockey team moves through the front door, cheers ring out. Patrons stand on chairs, toss back shots, and whistle, while calling out their gratitude for the win.

The space is well-worn and well-loved. Big, wooden planks crisscross the floor and neon signs light up the walls. It's got a familiar, neighborhood vibe to it, not unlike the places Henry took me to in Tennessee.

I like it immediately and Dec knows because he grips my fingers and shoots me a grin. He guides me through the crowd, keeping me in front of him, his fingers linked through the belt loops of my jeans.

"Hey Pete!" He waves to the bartender. "Back good?"

"It's yours," the bartender replies. "Nice game."

"Thanks." Dec leads the way to a back room that's empty but quickly fills with the team, their families, and some friends. Declan shifts us to the bar and cages me in, shadowing my back, as some of his teammates jostle next to us. His lips graze my ear and a chill rushes over my skin. "What're you drinking, babe?"

I push back into him, feeling the strength of his arms, the weight of his body hovering over mine. I like the feel of him pressed up against me. I like being with him again like this. I turn my head, the tip of my nose running along his jaw. He inhales sharply and I feel it down to my toes. The zap, the pull, whatever you want to call it, Declan and I've always had it.

"Margarita, rocks, extra salt."

He chuckles low, leaning closer to the bar. "Hey Selina, we'll take a margarita on the rocks with extra salt and an IPA."

"You got it." The bartender waves before grabbing a pint glass and filling Declan's beer.

"You ready to party?" Claire bumps into us from the side. Her blue eyes dance and she looks as excited as I feel.

"Yes," I tell her decisively.

She grins and wiggles her ass, before flagging down Selina. When the bartender turns, another one of Declan's teammates appears, clapping his hand over Claire's mouth as he calls out an order of tequila shots and slides his credit card across the bar.

"Panda!" Claire elbows him in the ribs. "I said I got shots tonight."

Panda rolls his eyes. "Yeah, okay, Claire."

I watch their easy exchange, note how Easton orders a

club soda with lemon, grin at how Abbi slips an arm around Claire's waist. Not for the first time, I acknowledge how much the Hawks are truly a family. They've gone out of their way to make me feel welcome and included. They've been nothing but supportive of Declan's and my union, unexpected as it may be. And I love that they've made me one of their own.

Turning in Declan's arms, I let the ledge of the bar cut into my back so I can gaze up at the man I now call husband.

"You ready to party?" I ask him.

Surprise glances off his lips but then he grins and lowers his face to mine.

"Careful, Vivi, you're giving me flashbacks of before."

I giggle. "I like the way we were before."

Declan's eyes darken, awareness flaring in their depths. "Me too, babe." He brushes a quick kiss over my lips as Selina lines up tequila shots behind me. "And yeah, I'm ready to fucking party with you."

CHAPTER 13
DECLAN

"**S**he's something else," Chloe says next to me at the bar.

I glance at my captain's girl and nod. "She's the best thing that ever happened to me."

My honesty surprises us both but once the words are out, I don't regret sharing them. Vivi has always been the greatest thing in my life, rivaling even hockey, and I've never been ashamed to admit that. While other guys were pulling the player card or telling girls one thing in private and fronting in public, I've always been all about Vivi. Until she broke my heart, and I went off to college angry, with a chip on my shoulder.

But now that I know the reason behind her disappearing act that summer, I feel guilty as fuck. Guilty and so damn disappointed in myself.

"I love this song!" Vivi waves her arms in the air, dancing her ass off with Claire and a happily intoxicated and recently engaged Indy.

"Me too!" Claire agrees, slapping Indy's ass.

Chloe snickers. "I'm so happy for Indy and Noah."

I nod, my eyes glued to my girl and the curves she's rocking. I love seeing her like this, uninhibited, caught up in the moment. This is the Vivi I remember. This is the girl I first fell in love with. She wore her heart on her sleeve and treated every moment like an adventure. She was bright and bubbly and enthusiastic about absolutely everything. Like the song that plays next and the chilled Patron shot Panda places in her hand.

"I know your wedding was…not what you expected," Chloe says next to me. My neck swivels toward her. "But you and Genevieve, you've got the same look in your eyes that Indy and Noah have. You've got that energy, that pull, between you guys. From an outsider looking in, you've got the kind of love that most people dream for."

I take a swig of my beer, unsure how to react to her observations. While I haven't been forthcoming with the strange details surrounding Vivi's and my marriage, I know it was a surprise to everyone. But more than that, does Vivi look at me with the kind of adoration Chloe hints at? Does she see me the same way I see her, the same way I've always seen her?

"Thanks, Chlo," I say finally.

Chloe pats me on the back. "I'm going to grab Austin. We've got my Mimi's birthday brunch tomorrow morning."

"Have fun," I say, wrapping an arm around her shoulder and giving her a side-hug goodbye.

Then I lean back against the bar, drink my beer, and watch my girl. By the third song, I'm desperate to get out of Taps too. I want to scoop Vivi up and take her home. I want to kiss her reckless and wake up to her in my bed.

But seeing how much fun she's having, watching her really enjoy her time with the girls holds me back. Until she glances up, her eyes connect with mine, and her mouth softens. Then all bets are off and I march my ass over to her, wrap her in my arms and whisper, "You're killing me, Vivi. Let's go home."

Her eyes spark as they meet mine. "Home?"

"You've always been my home."

She smiles. "You've always been mine too. I'm ready."

I wait as she says goodbye to the girls. I let my teammates know we're heading out. Then I hurry my girl to the car and drive us home.

Vivi is chatty on the ride.

"Did you know Claire designed the latest album cover for *The Burn Clovers*? And Indy's going to dress Emmaline up in the sweetest baby flower-girl dress. Maybe it will be a christening gown if they marry this year. I don't know. And Abbi asked if I'd want to help with some fundraiser she's running next month, which, obviously I said yes. Also, I need to send Indy a discount code I saw for hair extensions in case she wants to wear them for the wedding. Remind me, okay?"

I laugh, planting my palm on her thigh. She turns to look at me. Still rocking my jersey, her hair plaited into two braids, her face fresh and open, she almost looks like I remember. A younger, happier version of the woman I first stumbled upon in church. "I like seeing you like this."

She rolls her eyes but she's grinning.

"I'm serious. The past few weeks, you've been so serious. So caught up in your head, your work. It's nice to see you relax and have some fun," I continue.

"And make friends," she agrees.

"They're pretty great girls."

Vivi nods. "Sometimes I wish I went to college. Nights like these, I realize how much I missed out on. Other than trips with my dad, I never went anywhere outside of Tennessee."

I glance at her, noting the seriousness in her expression. "Do you still want to? Go to college, I mean?"

She shrugs, looking out the window. "I don't know. It seems too late now."

"It's not."

Vivi sighs. "After that summer, I kind of lost my footing. All of a sudden, going away seemed scary. The adventure part of it got lost in all the feelings I was sorting through. Granddaddy recognized it and threw me a lifeline—"

"The foundation."

She turns and smiles. "Yeah. I dove in and in many ways, the work there saved me. It gave me a purpose, a reason to show up at the office. The women I met, when I learned their stories and the losses they experienced, the sacrifices they made, well, my own experience paled in comparison."

I frown, my jaw tightening. Just because Vivi didn't have the same experiences as other women doesn't make her ordeal less valid. Less painful.

"No." Vivi holds out a hand. "It was good for me. The perspective, I mean. I needed it. So, I stayed home. Slowly, I carved out this future that worked. And I settled into it."

"And now?"

"Now, I'm making up for lost time with us. And I'm settling into my new life, with you. And, I really had fun tonight. Thanks for inviting me to your game." She smiles, her face so damn radiant that I feel it like a slap to the face.

"Baby, it's a standing invite. If we're going to make a go of this…"

"Like, for more than this year?" She wrinkles her nose.

Yes! I want to yell. For always.

But I don't want to scare her away, not when she's still coming to terms with so many changes, and still finding her footing in Boston.

So, I shoot her a smirk. "I never wanted a future with anyone but you, Vivi. Maybe things just have a way of working out."

"Maybe," she agrees, but her smile widens and her eyes shine.

I park the SUV and take her hand as we make our way up to my apartment.

"Do you want to redecorate our bedroom?" I ask, the words out of my mouth before I can stop them. "You can order whatever you want."

"We'll see," she says, and since it's not a no, I let it go. I unlock the door and follow Vivi inside.

Halfway to our bedroom, Vivi turns toward me, her expression playful. Expectant.

"What is it?" I ask.

She sucks in a breath and gazes up at me from underneath long eyelashes. And I *know*.

"I'm taking too long?" I guess.

She smirks, biting the corner of her mouth.

"Sleeping next to me is too hard and you want my body?" I continue, moving toward her.

Now she's laughing openly.

I tug on one of her braids, lifting her face to mine.

"I want you, Vivi. God, do I want you. But if we do this, I want to know you're all in, the same way I am."

Her inhale is sharp, her eyes wide. "Yes. Dec, I want this, with you." She gestures between us.

Relief mixed with an edge of surprise rocks through me. "Baby," I murmur, my hand slipping to her ass and pressing her body against mine. "More than anything in the world, I want this with you too." I walk her backward, through the doorway to the bedroom. "Tonight, seeing you in my number, watching you with the team, Vivi, I—"

Her mouth crashes over mine as she vaults herself into my arms. I grab her ass before she can fall and we tilt forward, the two of us landing in the center of the bed, with my one hand cradling her head.

"Sorry," she laughs. The sound cuts through my chest because it's so sweet and familiar and...God, how have I lived the last seven years of my life without this woman?

Vivi tugs me down by my shirt and then, she's kissing me

and I'm kissing her back, pressing her frame into the mattress.

"Wait, how drunk are you?" I murmur.

She shakes her head. "Not drunk at all. I didn't take the last two shots Panda gave me. I just feel…alive."

Thank God. She pops the button on her jeans and I tug on the cuffs until her pants are discarded on the floor. I pull my shirt over my head and stare down at her, all creamy skin wrapped up in my number. My team. My jersey.

"Jesus, Vivi," I mutter, folding forward until my hands plant on either side of her head. "I've dreamed of you like this."

Her breath catches and her expression suddenly turns serious. The giggling of a moment ago is gone. "Dec, I…"

"Tell me."

Her legs come up in response and hook around my lower back. "It's only ever been like this with you."

I pause, trying to understand the meaning of her words. "But you've been with other guys…since us, right?"

She blushes, her lower lip locked between her teeth. The sassy girl I was getting a glimpse of has become real serious, real nervous, real fast. "Yes," she admits, "but I've never, they've never…" She closes her eyes. "I've never orgasmed with them. I've never felt…everything, the way I do with you."

I groan. "Jesus, Vivi. You're going to kill me." I lower myself slowly. While our past kisses were needy or playful, this one is different. It's so slow and sexy, it's agonizing.

My hand spans the side of her face, my pinky by her ear, my thumb tracing her lower lip. I slant my mouth over hers and pour my apologies, my desires, my truths into her mouth like years haven't passed between us. I kiss her like she's still mine and in so many ways, in every way that matters, she is.

"Genevieve," I murmur, kissing the underside of her jaw.

She arches into me, a whimper falling from her mouth. "I don't, I can't," she sputters.

I pause and pull back to stare at her. "Tell me anything, babe. Everything."

Embarrassment blazes over her face. "I don't know how to do this anymore," she whispers, sweet as fuck. "With you."

"My Vivi." I brush my fingers over her plump mouth, shiny from my kiss. "Just feel, baby. Just feel and be here with me. You don't have to do anything. We'll figure it all out together." Her eyes bore into mine, hopeful and vulnerable. All I want to do is fill them with trust, with a confidence in me, in us. "We can go as slow or as fast as you want. We don't have to do this at all." I gesture between us.

She shakes her head. "No, I want this, Dec. God, I want you. I've been thinking about this for weeks."

"You have?"

"Yeah. I just, I'm scared it won't be…good for you. I know you've been, well, living life and I've just been in Nashville, trying to move forward but never enough to feel again." She fumbles with her words, her cheeks red, her neck flushed.

"Don't you get it, Vivi? There is no one for me but you. Being with you right now makes me hate the fact that I've ever been with anyone else. But I can swear to you, nothing from my past has ever measured up to you. No one. I want everything, baby, and I feel so damn grateful for whatever you're willing to give me."

Her eyes widen at my admission and I chuckle.

"I need to do a better job telling you how I feel," I admit, settling more firmly in between her thighs. "I just don't want to scare you off."

"Scare me off?" she repeats, confused. "Dec, I've been mostly numb since you left. And now, it's like this blazing heat, trying to live in a damn inferno. I don't want to be cold anymore."

"I hate that you had to deal with so much on your own. I wish I had been there. I never would have left if—"

"Shh, just kiss me. Make me feel." Her voice is thicker than it was a moment ago and seeing the need she speaks about flare in her eyes, I do as she says.

I drop my head, capture her lips, and blaze a fire that consumes us both.

CHAPTER 14
VIVI

Declan's kiss infuses me with the same things as when I was twelve: hope and heart and heat. For a blink, we're kids again, fumbling though this kissing thing. And then, we're very much adults, touching, exploring, and feeling too many things at once.

Declan's hands are tentative over my skin, unsure how much to give or take. But when his hand travels up my shirt and his fingers brush over my breast, I literally moan and press up into his palm, desperate for more.

That's the signal that clues him in and he wastes no time rolling my nipple between his expert fingers. My hands drop to his pants, and I manage to get them down over his hips before he kicks them off. When he's in boxers and I'm rocking his jersey, I revel in the feel of his legs tangling up with mine.

He boxes me in, his arms bracketing off the outside world so all I see is him. And what else is there to see anyway? His gray eyes are hazy with desire, his stubble is rough against my skin, and his mouth is damn hot when it fuses with mine.

He works the jersey up to my neckline, swearing when he gets a full look at my breasts, straining against the delicate, lace demi cups of my bra. I may not have had much action in recent years, but I've always worn sexy lingerie sets for myself. They infused me with a confidence, an edge, that I often needed.

"This is hot," Dec says, hooking a finger around a bra strap and dragging it down my shoulder. His fingers flutter over the top of my chest, dipping down in between my breasts. His eyes meet mine for a blink and so slowly my breath catches, he lowers his head, tugs down the cup of the bra, and takes my breast in between his lips.

"Oh," I sigh.

His tongue drags over my nipple and I close my eyes, relishing his touch. As he drags his mouth to my other breast, the friction of his stubble sliding over my skin lights me up and I wrap my legs around his hips. As I pull him toward me, his hard length rubs against my core and we both groan.

He's rock hard against me and I'm suddenly desperate to touch him, to feel him, the same way he touches me as his fingers deftly slip inside my panties. He sucks on my nipple as his fingers part me and at the warmth that pools in my core, I know I'm already soaking wet for him. For this.

"Vivi, fuck. Baby, you're dripping," he mutters, moving down my body. His words cause my cheeks to blaze but not enough for me to stop him. No, right now, I want Declan and his magical fingers more than I want air.

I shimmy out of my bra as he drags my panties down my legs. Bare and spread out beneath Declan is an experience I've missed out on for far too long.

His eyes drink me in slowly, lingering on every inch of my skin like I'm a rare piece of art, something he won't ever be able to appreciate again. His breathing ticks up and even though I thought it was impossible, he grows even harder. My lips part as he loses his boxers, his cock springing free.

Declan is kneeling to my side, watching me as I watch him. The space between us crackles with electricity and heat. It's more intense than anything I've ever experienced, and I literally moan as he palms his cock, dragging his hand over the shaft and slowly pumping.

"You're the most gorgeous woman I've ever seen, Vivi." His voice is rough, raspy. Sexy.

I work a swallow, my throat dry, my thighs tumbling. "Dec. I love you." The words pop out, unbidden, but too true to deny.

His eyes spring to mine and his whole face softens at whatever he reads in my expression. Tears, desperate, relieved, happy tears collect in my eyes.

Declan shifts over me, his index finger sliding underneath my right eye. "Don't cry, baby. I love you too. I love you so fucking much."

I wrap my hand around his wrist. "I'm just so…relieved. I never thought, I never even let myself believe, that I could feel like this again."

Declan's eyes bore into mine with a seriousness, a possessiveness, that I fall forward into. "Well get ready to feel like this every day for the rest of our lives. I love you, my beautiful girl. I love you and I never stopped."

I smile, his words healing some of the cracks I've carried around since he left.

"Make love to me, Dec?"

"Every damn day, Vivi." He lowers over me slowly.

My legs encircle his hips, his mouth finds mine, and so slowly it's better than I've ever dreamed, Declan loves me.

He tastes every inch of my skin. He drags his body down mine. His tongue finds my core, slick and trembling for his touch, and I cry out, my fingers gripping his curls.

He laps at my clit, little tastes that cause my stomach to clench, before he sucks me into his mouth and I buck against him, shattering within seconds. If it wasn't Declan, I'd be embarrassed. But everything about this moment feels right, natural, necessary.

So I let him gather me to his chest, kissing my face and

neck as he rolls on a condom. I wrap myself around him and shudder as he enters me for the first time in seven years.

"You okay, baby?" He moves slowly, rocking into me one inch at a time.

I let out a slow exhale, focusing on relaxing enough to accept him as he stretches me to the limit. "Yes," I say, delicious tingles shooting through my body as he twitches inside of me. "I'm so good, Dec." I grip his shoulders.

He shoots me a look filled with such genuine happiness that I grin, feeling the same delight swell in my chest. Then, Declan begins to move and my eyes fall closed, every sensation under the sun flowing through me with enough intensity to wipe out the loneliness I've wrapped myself in these past seven years.

Declan brings me to the peak again and I swear, hearing his surprised laughter for one beat, until he cries out and follows me. We crash down together, our slick bodies rubbing against each other as Dec collapses next to me. He pulls me against his chest as my thighs rub together, wet from my own arousal.

Declan kisses the back of my neck. "That was...everything. You're fucking everything."

I turn in his arms, kissing his lips. "You're my home, Dec."

"Always, Vivi," he says seriously.

I smile softly, his lips curl upwards, and we stare at each other, memorizing the curves and lines of each other's faces until we both drop into a sweet slumber.

WAKING in Declan's bed after a night of smoking hot sex feels better than anything I've ever experienced. It's pure peace of mind. Whatever worries I had no longer exist. Whatever reservations I conjured up have been obliterated.

As if the past seven years never happened, it's me and Dec again. He stretches his gloriously naked body out and I spend time appreciating it before his eyes flick up to mine.

"I see you checking me out," he laughs.

I shrug. "Not trying to hide it, Dec."

He grins, his arm hooking around my waist and dragging me to him. "Morning, baby girl."

"Morning," I say, kissing him.

While I expect him to pull away and head out for a run the way he does every morning, he shifts his weight until his body covers mine. He kisses me hard and I quickly return the sentiment, meeting him nip for nip.

Declan's hands find mine, our fingers threading together. He moves our arms above my head, pressing my hands into the pillow. We kiss like it's been months and not hours since we've enjoyed each other.

Since we're already naked, it only takes moments to have us both panting, our hands tracing each other's bodies. Declan grabs a condom from his bedside drawer, and I do my best not to think of all the women he's had in this bed before me. Before I can spend too much time trying to redirect my thoughts, he does it for me.

He passes me the condom, rolls over, and hauls me up, until I'm straddling his abdomen. His abs freaking wink at me, rippling and dancing as he shifts. "You rival high school you," I tell him.

He snorts, his hand gripping my hip. "What's that mean?"

I drag my fingers over his abs, loving how they move under my touch. "Never seen abs like this."

"I'll do more sit-ups," he swears.

I laugh.

He lifts his chin toward the condom. "Your turn, baby. Do whatever you want to me. I'm yours."

I glance at him skeptically, wondering if he knows how out of my depth I am. Sure, I've had sex before, but I always let the guy take the lead.

His expression softens and he wraps his hands over mine, the packaging of the condom crinkling. "When we used to be together, we were both kind of fumbling along. Exploring things for the first time."

I nod.

"You don't need to be embarrassed with me. If you're curious, try it. I want to learn what you like and I'm not sure if you've learned that for yourself yet. So, I'm yours. Move however you want, do whatever you like. Let's learn together."

I know I blush from his words but at the steadiness in his tone, the confidence in his body as he lays out, unashamed and unabashed by his own nakedness, I do as he says.

I drop the condom next to us on the bed. I plant my hand on his hard pecs and I lower myself to take his mouth. I slant my lips over his, drinking greedily. When I'm ready, I track my hands down his body. He's already hard, twitching for my touch. This morning, with the sunlight streaming in, I wrap my hand around him and pump his shaft the same way I watched him do last night. Flipping my eyes up to his, I note the haziness that spreads through his irises, the uptick in his breathing. He watches me lazily, a smile spreading over his face, before he bites his lower lip and gasps.

"Feels good, baby." His words encourage me to move faster.

Declan's fingers wrap around my lower leg and hold tightly. Knowing that I'm turning him on, I lower my mouth to his cock and lick a trail up the shaft, his skin like silk against my tongue.

"Jesus," he mutters.

I grin. Then, I wrap my lips around him and begin to bob,

taking my time to listen for his verbal cues, to feel the way his body responds under my touch.

Declan's fingers twist in my hair, tugging. His breathing grows erratic, and his thighs tighten beneath me. When he growls I let him slip from my mouth with a pop. I grab the condom, tear it open, and roll it over him.

All the while, his eyes stare at me, colored with lust. "You sure it's been that long? Because that was incredible."

I laugh, shaking my head. I situate myself over him, bracing my hands on his shoulders. He grips my hips to steady me while I lower myself over him.

When I'm root deep we both cry out. Then, I begin to move, finding my own rhythm, chasing my own orgasm. I close my eyes, shake my hair out, and tip my face to the sky as Declan pulses inside of me and I shatter around him, his name a prayer on my lips.

CHAPTER 15
DECLAN

"You look happy for someone who just missed the block," Panda calls out from behind me in goal.

I skate around and smirk at him. "Just making sure you get the practice you need."

He chuckles, lifting his glove in my direction. "Clearly you need it more than me."

I flip my chin before turning back around, gearing up for the next play. Practice is light since we have a game tomorrow. The lack of intensity means my mind is wandering more than usual.

Wandering all over Vivi's delicious body, her delicate curves and inspiring strength. Four days ago, I sunk into her for the first time in years and that connection felt just like the homecoming it was.

Who knew marriage could be this great? Who knew life could be so damn perfect?

A whistle blows. "Yaeger, get your damn head in the play," Coach hollers.

I dip my head and lift a hand in acknowledgement. Time to focus on hockey, but even that's been hard with Vivi around. I used to be so ambitious in my pursuit of the game, so singularly focused. And now, more often than not, my head is caught up on her. On her past, on our future, on all the things in between.

The whistle sounds again, and I crouch down, forcing myself to zero in on the puck. Practice lasts for another twenty minutes, and I make sure I'm mentally present for all of them. But the lightness in my body, the happiness flowing through me, doesn't fade.

After I shower off and enter the locker room, I see Easton and Austin are still around.

When East spots me, he snickers. "Hey there, loverboy."

"You better cut that shit out before tomorrow," Austin reprimands. "We're all happy for you that things between you and Genevieve are solid, but—"

"Don't take the ice with your fucking bedroom eyes again. I'm gonna puke if I have to witness that expression cross your face one more time," East explains.

I flip them the bird, but I received their message. Loud and clear. Sims and I used to joke about how whipped Scotch is or how lame Austin got and yet, here I am, unable to focus on practice, because I'm thinking about my girl. No wonder Sims has barely spoken to me since I came back from Tennessee.

But Easton and Austin don't look surprised.

"You go on a honeymoon yet?" Austin asks.

"What?" I glance at him.

East snaps his fingers and points at me. "You need to go away for a night."

I laugh. "Go away? We're in the middle of the season."

"You can do a staycation." He shrugs.

"Or a night in Martha's Vineyard. Chloe and I went last summer and—"

"He got lucky as a motherfucker," East explains.

Austin smacks him on the back of the neck, his face reddening.

"It's a nice place," Austin says.

I pause, thinking their suggestion over. "We haven't had any real time together. Just dinners and watching Netflix," I admit.

"Netflix and chill," Easton mutters under his breath.

Austin sighs, as if Easton's childish antics are annoying him when we all know they've been best friends for ages. "Listen, we need you on the ice. With your head in the game. I get that you're newly married and I'm happy for you, that things are going so well after a ..."

"Rough start," East supplies.

I grin.

"So do us all a favor and take your girl away for a night. Do whatever—"

"Romantic bullshit," East interrupts.

"Whatever you need to do," Austin continues. "And then show up to every game for the rest of the season ready to play."

"I'll think about it," I say, not admitting that it's a really good idea. I'd love to get Vivi out of our routine and do something fun with her. Take a walk on the beach. Even though it's still too cold to properly enjoy it, I might be able to convince her to wear a bikini. We could hang out, spend time together, be a real...couple.

And, considering we're in season and hopefully going to make the play-offs, Martha's Vineyard is conceivable.

After I say goodbye to the guys, I walk to my SUV. Along the way, I check my calendar, pick next Thursday as a good choice, and call to make a reservation to surprise my girl. As far as husband gifts go, mine have been severely lacking.

"NICE BLOCK, YAEGER!" Scotch hollers out as he skates past me.

I grin, knowing I'm having one of my best performances this season. More than that, my girl is here witnessing it all. East and Austin were right, as soon as I booked Martha's Vineyard, as soon as I planned to spend some quality time with Vivi, I've been able to focus.

We head to the beach next week and right now, I'm all in on this game. The center for Tampa barrels toward me and I skate backwards, determined not to let him get a clear shot on goal.

He attempts a fake, snapping the puck across to line up for a shot but I catch a piece of it. As soon as my stick collides with the puck, I'm maneuvering my body weight to get a clear pass to East.

Pass completed, East takes off, pulling off a deke that gives him an open shot. He takes it, dropping the puck in the top right-hand corner of the net.

The crowd goes nuts, chanting his name as he pulls off a glory shot. East turns toward me and lifts his arm and I flip my chin up at him. Grinning, I get back into my position. But before play resumes, I chance a glance at my girl.

She's on her feet, clapping and cheering so loudly that a burst of pride explodes in my chest.

Thank you, Mr. Harrison. Not only did you give me hockey, but you gave me a shot with Vivi.

Knowing what a lucky bastard I am, I focus back on the game. But when we win, I'm taking my girl straight home, skipping Taps, to have her all to myself.

"YOU WERE INCREDIBLE!" Vivi gushes as I close the door to our condo.

"Having you there pushed me to show off."

She laughs. "Yeah right. Want a drink? An icepack? Food?"

"Just you, baby," I tell her the truth.

She spins around, still shuffling backward but at the seriousness in my expression, her smile widens. "You already have me, Yaeger."

"Yaeger." I chuckle, advancing on her.

"Number four." She rolls her leggings down and kicks them to the side. Clad in my number, her legs bare, has me quickening my pace.

"I like seeing you wear it." I catch her, my hands connecting with her hips.

"I bet," she murmurs, but her eyes flare with heat. She stops backing away and stands still, tipping her chin up.

I dip down and kiss her, loving that she packs all her sass and spice into five feet four inches. Her hands unbuckle my belt, pop the button on my jeans. When her fingers slip under the hem of my shirt, I help her out and tug it clear off. She grins, placing her palms on my chest.

"I'm surprised you don't have any tattoos," she says.

I cock an eyebrow. "Really? I strike you as a tattoo guy? You know Da would have skinned my ass."

She laughs. "Yeah, then. But not now."

"What would you get?" I ask her, curious.

Her fingers reach for the pendant of Saint Genevieve that she wears around her neck. "Probably a candle," she says quietly. I already know the meaning behind it, that Saint Genevieve is always depicted with a candle, and her Mama named her Genevieve immediately after her birth, only moments before she passed. Understanding the connection to her mama, I don't press.

"Well, I'd get your name. Your whole name, Genevieve Rae, right over my heart."

Her laughter is instant. She shakes her head and taps her palm against my chest. "You're so lame."

"Just Vivi then?"

"No way." Her hands slide up to my shoulders and she grips hard, jumping up to wrap her legs around my waist.

I palm her ass, keeping her frame secure against mine. "You're the most important person in my life," I tell her truthfully, as I walk us into our bedroom.

I drop her on the bed, glancing around the space. It's still decorated in gray and shades of blue. "You know, if you want to redecorate, you can."

"I know." She smiles.

"Or we could move."

"Move?" Her eyebrows lift.

"To a bigger place," I suggest, knowing this condo must be crazy cramped after the estate, the mansion, she grew up on.

Vivi hooks her heels around the backs of my knees and tugs until I collapse over her. "Declan Yaeger, haven't you realized yet that you are my home. I don't care what color the duvet is or if we have two bathrooms or five. I just want to be with you."

I brush my hand over her hair, smoothing it back from her face. "I love you, Vivi."

"I love you, too. But I still don't want you to tattoo my name on your chest."

"What about my ass?" I joke.

She shoves at me, cracking up again, but then she's pulling me closer and I'm going. Willingly.

Making love to Vivi is akin to a transcendental experience.

It's the most powerful connection I've ever had and the most beautiful high I've ever experienced. Being with Genevieve again has changed the game for me.

And I want to live in our little corner of the world, the peaceful cocoon we've wrapped ourselves in, for as long as possible. For forever.

CHAPTER 16
VIVI

"What do you think?" I ask Declan as the realtor takes a phone call.

"I like this space better than the last one." He walks to the windows slowly, glancing down at the street. "I think you'll better serve the community in this location."

"I agree."

"But…" Declan turns toward me.

"But," I prompt.

"The kitchen at the other location would make having the food shelter component you talked about easier. Right from the start."

"True." I walk around the space.

We're viewing our third property. While I don't want to make any definitive plans until I have a better pulse on the needs of the community, I want to start learning about my options.

"I'm meeting with one of the directors at a women's shelter, Maybelle's House, tomorrow," I say, taking out my phone to snap some photos. This space is better situated but requires a lot of renovations from the get-go. Since everything in Boston is new, I'm hesitant to take on more than I can chew.

Especially with all the other programs the foundation is running. I slide my phone back into my pocket and bite my lip, thinking. Can I pull this off?

"Hey." Dec's hand lands on my shoulder.

I turn into him, and his fingers find purchase on my hips. "You've done an incredible job. Vivi, you've only been in town for two months. Give yourself some grace."

I grin at the phrase. *Give yourself some grace.* It's something Henry's mom used to say to us, and I like that Declan remembers it too.

"How are things going at the Harrison Foundation?" he asks.

"Good. With Alfred not in the way, my working relationships are solid. Everyone on the team has been open to new ideas, new approaches. We're still sorting out the best path forward. We're getting there."

Dec kisses the top of my head. "You're the baddest woman I know, Vivi."

I snort. "Yeah, get that tattooed on your ass."

He tosses his head back and laughs, the sound rumbly and hot.

I grin, pinching his side, as our realtor walks back into the space.

"What do you think?" he asks.

"I like it. I took some photos. Thank you for your time today. The properties we saw have given me some things to consider." I walk closer to him, extending my hand. "I'll be in touch."

He shakes my hand professionally. "Thank you, Genevieve. I'll keep an eye out for similar listings to send your way. If you have any questions, or anything I can help with, shoot me an email."

"Will do. Thanks."

I watch as the realtor leaves. Again, Declan shadows my back.

"You did good, baby."

"Thanks for coming today." I glance up at him.

"Anything you need," he reminds me, pressing a quick kiss to my lips. "I'm your guy."

"You're my guy all right," I agree, wrapping an arm around his waist and steering him out of the space so David can lock up after us. "Want to take me home and remind me?"

He scoffs but I catch the challenge mixed with desire that flares in his eyes. They turn charcoal, a color he wears well. "Remind you? I guess I'm not doing my job."

"I guess not," I lament, walking toward his SUV.

Dec smacks my ass and I turn to stick my tongue out at him.

"Get in the car." He points at the passenger door. "I'm going to take you home and make sure you never need another damn reminder again."

I giggle. "I'm counting on it, Dec."

"WAIT!" I push his shoulder, faking left before moving right around the couch.

Dec cracks up. "You are a little kid."

"Tell me more about the surprise!"

I round the back of the couch, waiting for his words, when he really surprises me by lunging over the couch and wrapping me in his arms.

"Argh!" I shriek.

Dec falls backward, over the back of the couch, and we land with an oomph on the cushions. He cradles me in his arms, his shoulders shaking with silent laughter. I push up on him and arch an eyebrow, trying to look stern, but I'm laughing too hard to pull it off.

"The surprise?" I ask again.

Dec smacks my ass and drags me closer to his mouth. "The surprise is, I'm taking you away."

"Away where? You made the play-offs!"

He smirks. "Hell yeah we did."

I roll my eyes.

"Away for one night. It's not far and it's not the trip you deserve but…baby, we never had a honeymoon. Jesus, we never even had a real date. Just dinner around town, half the time with the team."

"I like the team."

He kisses my nose. "I know you do. And I love that. But I want to spend time with my girl."

I beam at him, feeling very much the teenage version of myself. The girl who lost her virginity to the boy staring up at me with pure joy in his eyes. "What do I pack?"

"Bathing suit. Something sexy."

I chuckle and bite the corner of my mouth. Dec's hand reaches up and his thumb frees my bottom lip and swipes over my mouth.

"Jeans and a light sweater. A pair of shorts and shirt, in case we take a hike."

"A hike?" I repeat, skeptical.

He taps my ass again. "You'll like this place. It's the kind of place you want to spend outdoors."

I grin, thinking of those Tennessee summers spent horsing around, hiking and swimming. "Okay. Anything else?"

"Maybe a dress?"

I spread my fingers over his chest, loving the hard muscle that presses against my palm. "Definitely a dress." I lower my face and kiss his lips. "You gonna give me any more hints?"

"Nope." He smiles. "Just be ready to go, Thursday morning, at 7 a.m."

"Seven?"

"Hell yeah, baby. If I only get one day with you before hockey takes over my life, I'm gonna take it all."

"Seven," I confirm. Then I roll off him and wiggle my ass until he laughs.

"Where are you going?" he groans.

"Girls' lunch." I waltz into our bedroom and change into a pair of jeans. Then I grab my mama's coat and purse.

"Again?" Dec's voice carries from the living room.

I grin at the exasperation in his tone. While Declan's been busy with practices, team meetings, and watching game tapes at Easton's, I've been cultivating my own social circle with Claire, Abbi, Chloe, and the rest of the BHH girls.

I spend a few minutes in the bathroom, touching up my makeup and clipping the front of my hair away from my face. Then I pop in some earrings, spritz my favorite perfume, and head back into the living room.

Dec is sitting on the couch now, his arms crossed over his chest. I can tell he's trying to look annoyed but he's losing the battle because his face is reddening from holding back his laughter.

"Jealous?" I ask.

His eyes scan my body, lingering over my legs. "You have no idea."

I wrinkle my nose. He smirks and stands from the couch. Walking over to me, he kisses the top of my head. "Have fun. If it turns into a boozy lunch, call me for a ride."

"Don't you have practice?" I turn in his arms, loving the way they feel wrapped around me. Loving the way he cages me in between the kitchen island and his frame.

Even though it's only been a handful of weeks, my relationship with Declan has centered me. I feel like I'm back on my path again, blazing forward in everything, when I was wary of a romantic relationship for so long.

"I do." He brushes a kiss over my cheek. "But then I'll be

chilling at East's. I take it Claire will be at this lunch?" He kisses my other cheek.

"Yes." I tip my chin up and kiss his lips. "But Abbi's driving since Claire and I don't have cars."

He pulls back slightly. "Do you want a car?"

"When I decided I'm ready to maneuver these city streets, I'll buy one."

"Or I could buy one for you."

I shake my head. "No, thanks. You already pay for our entire lifestyle. Our condo." I toss my hand out to the side.

He turns and glances around the kitchen and living room. "We still need a bigger place."

I shake my head, resting my palm on his chest. "Already told you, just need you."

He grins, his eyes like ink when they meet mine. Soft and shining. "Me too."

My phone buzzes in the back pocket of my jeans and I pull it out to read the message. "Abbi's on her way."

"All right. Have fun at lunch, baby."

"See you later, Dec." I give him a quick kiss. Then I stuff my phone into my purse and head downstairs to wait for Abbi.

When I push out into the sunshine, it's breezy but with a clear blue sky, and I inhale deeply. I never thought I'd live in a city. I never thought my life would take such a drastic change. In fact, for the past seven years I couldn't imagine my future outside of the foundation at all.

I lift my face to the sunshine, close my eyes, and smile.

It's so much better than I ever considered. Being with Declan again is everything.

Salt and sea and sunshine hang heavy in the air as I cradle Vivi between my arms. Her face is tipped upward, her eyes closed, the rush of wind blowing her hair back into my face.

"This is peaceful," she murmurs as we take the ferry from Boston to Martha's Vineyard.

Chloe and Austin helped me plan the logistics of our overnight since they celebrated a wedding here last summer. While taking my car was certainly an option, I wanted to soak up every bit of this experience with Vivi. And the ferry, sans car, won out.

"You cold?" I step closer, until my chest presses into her back.

She turns to grin at me over her shoulder, strands of her hair sticking to her lip gloss.

I tug them free as she shakes her head. "No, I'm great."

"Good."

She turns in my arms, and I lower my face, kissing her as the ferry pulls into the harbor at Oak Bluffs.

As we disembark from the ferry, Vivi's gaze darts everywhere. The smile on her face is priceless and I love her enthusiasm.

"Wow," she breathes. "Look at these adorable gingerbread houses!" She points to the quaint cottages lining the streets in vibrant colors. Cotton candy pinks, flashy teals, and sunny yellows greet us, and I puff up with relief that Chloe encouraged me to rent one of these small houses.

Even though it's only for one night, she assured me that the privacy will be nice and that Vivi would love the sweet, cottage experience. Since I hired a private chef for dinner and arranged for the house to be fully stocked, as if we were staying at a hotel, I have to agree. Chloe Crawford was spot on.

"I'm glad you like them so much, because we're staying at one down this street." I clasp her hand, our overnight bag thrown over my shoulder, as we turn down a side street, boasting more inviting cottages.

When we stop in front of number forty-two, Vivi sighs. "This is perfect, Dec."

I stand beside her, staring up at the compact, shingled cottage, complete with a porch and hanging lanterns. It's white, blue, and pink and something I never thought I'd ever spend a night in until this moment. Now, I can't wait to get my girl inside and never leave.

"Can we go for a bike ride?" She points to a couple riding past on bikes.

I chuckle, forcing down my ideas at getting her naked in a bedroom. Or the kitchen. Hell, even the beach.

"Yeah, Vivi. We can go for a bike ride."

She beams.

I guide her inside, surprised at how modern the remodel is. The space is small but clean and everything is white and wood. It's the perfect little getaway.

"This is so sweet!" Vivi exclaims, running through the space like a kid.

I shake my head and lean back against the kitchen island, watching her. A lightness I'm not used to fills my chest. I feel relaxed and at ease, which is not the norm since I'm gearing up for the play-offs.

Right now, I just want to get lost with my girl and act like tourists, together in this beautiful, peaceful corner of the world we've never been to before.

"How'd they know I love peach sparkling water?" Vivi wonders, pulling two cans from the fridge and tossing me one.

I catch it and pop the tab. "You happy, my Vivi?"

She pulls her blonde waves into a ponytail, and I love that it's lopsided.

"I can't believe you did all this, Dec. This is...I don't remember the last time I took a break. A time out."

"Me neither," I admit, realizing it's been at least two years since I've been to the beach. "Bike rides?"

"Definitely. I saw a lighthouse on the way in."

"Yeah, babe. But that's over fifteen miles of biking."

Vivi wrinkles her nose.

"Come on." I hold out my hand. "Let's go walk on the beach, grab some bikes, and see where the day leads us."

She ties a hoodie around her waist and places her hand in mine. "I'm ready."

"YOU'RE DRIPPING IT EVERYWHERE!" Vivi accuses, passing me a wad of napkins as some of my rocky road ice cream lands on her knee. Then, her hand.

I grip her hand in mine and lick the ice cream off her thumb.

She rolls her eyes and pulls her hand away but she's

laughing. It's the best sound in the world, especially with the soundtrack of ocean waves and seagulls in the background.

Vivi's eyes dance as they hold mine. She takes a healthy lick of her strawberry ice cream, dipped in chocolate sprinkles, and moans. "This is the best ice cream I've ever had."

I snort, tossing the wad of napkins back at her.

"I'm serious. It must be the ocean." She looks out to the sea.

I follow her gaze, stretching my legs out in front of me as we watch the waves roll in. We've been biking for the past hour, weaving in and out of inviting side streets and down stretches of grassy farmland. Now, we're back by the beach, watching kite surfers dance along the tops of waves and listening to the giggles of children filling buckets with sand.

"It's supposed to heal all wounds," I comment.

Vivi glances at me. "I thought that was time."

I lace my fingers with her sticky ones. Looking at her, I say truthfully, "Maybe it's a combination of both."

Her expression softens, some of the playfulness turning into a quiet reflection. "Maybe."

"I'm happy we're married, Vivi. I know this wasn't planned but I only ever wanted to be your husband. I knew it as a high school kid and even then, I knew how rare that was. To find your person so early on in life."

"I always knew it too."

Dropping a kiss to the top of her head, I say, "Now we're together, Vivi. No matter what happens from here on out, I'll always find you."

She squints up at me, her expression gauging the seriousness of my words. But I one hundred percent mean them. I mean everything I say to her.

"I love you, Declan Yaeger."

"Love you more, Genevieve Rae."

We smile at each other and it's as if we're the only two

people on this beach, on Martha's Vineyard, on planet Earth who know this secret. Our secret.

For two motherless kids who both lost their footing, we're doing okay. Vivi and I are blazing our own path, finding our future, in each other and together.

There's no greater achievement than that and as I witness the continuous flow of the ocean, tide rolling in, tide going out, I'm grateful to have Vivi by my side.

"THERE'S MORE!" She gasps, her eyes running over the delicious dinner spread out along the kitchen island.

The private chef I hired has been in constant communication with me, which is how I knew to arrive home now. He left about three minutes ago and as I take in the perfect dishes he created, all adorned with cards describing the dish, I admit he was worth every penny. And then some.

Since I elected for Vivi and I to eat on our own, the chef prepared a bunch of tasting dishes for us to eat at our leisure instead of a formal meal with set courses.

"Oysters." I waggle my eyebrows.

Vivi swats me in the stomach.

"Clams," she continues, pointing out the dishes. "Lobster. And what's this…" She gets closer to one of the entrees. "Wild mushroom truffle gnocchi," she moans, reading the little place card. "Ooh, I love this. Are these truffle fries?"

My stomach growls, and she laughs.

"All that's left to do is light the candles and pour the wine." I pick up the chardonnay, already sitting in an ice chiller.

Vivi lights the candles, we take our seats, and I pass her a glass of wine.

"Cheers, baby." I lift my glass.

"To us." She smiles that stunning smile, the one that makes her face light up like the North Star. The one I keep falling more and more in love with.

Our glasses clink together and a peaceful kind of steadiness rolls through me. I've never been so certain of my direction, my purpose before. But now that Vivi is back in my life and we're making a real go of our future, I've also never been so happy.

CHAPTER 18
VIVI

Moonlight ripples over his expression, simultaneously casting him in shadows and illuminating the planes of his face. His eyes burn hotter than I've ever seen them. Pewter and iron orbs reflecting more love than I've ever known.

He lays me down, naked and wanting, in the center of our bed, the small room cocooning us in, keeping us sheltered in our little slice of reality. Ooh, Declan Yaeger is more than I ever anticipated. My body yearns for his touch, for his heat, for all the absolutions his lips press into my skin.

"I love the way you look at me," I tell him truthfully. The way Declan looks at me makes me feel more than beautiful. He makes me feel whole.

"Better be the only man lookin' at you like this," he replies, his mouth moving down my neck.

I arch into him as his fingertips glide up my calf until he grips the back of my knee and fastens my leg around his hip. His weight settles over me, pressing me into the mattress. My eyes are already closed, my body lost to the sensations he easily pulls from it. My hands track his naked back and I relish the feel of his shoulder blades, all sinewy strength, moving beneath my palms.

"Dec," I whimper as his mouth fastens over my nipple, teasing.

He's already rock solid, his cock teasing other parts of my body.

"Please," I murmur.

"Shh." His stubble is delicious as it glides over my stomach, then lower. "Let me make this good for you, baby."

"You are. You always do," I plead, needing more of him.

His tongue flicks over my clit and I see stars. "Dec," I repeat, nearly chanting his name as he works me over. My hands grasp at pillows, at bedding, at anything to root myself to this moment as my body tightens, a powerful hum that grows louder, more intense, until I cry out and shatter against his mouth.

Dec doesn't give me a moment to recover. No. His mouth trails over my inner thighs, nipping and kissing. His fingers roll my nipples. His body over mine, moving, taking, and giving is more erotic than anything I've ever seen.

"Please, baby," I beg.

He grins, looking so damn satisfied with himself that I soften even more, liquid heat flooding my limbs.

"Let me grab a condom." He makes to move off the bed.

Faster than lightning, my legs clamp around him, holding him in place. "No. I want you. I'm on the shot and I'm clean."

He pauses, his eyes wide. "You sure, Vivi?"

"Dec, we're married."

He chuckles. "I know. And I'm clean too." He gathers me to his chest and enters me swiftly, fully, the feeling so intense that we both groan.

We move at the same time, in sync. Our bodies make music, a symphony of movement that brings us both to the peak, over and over again. But we hold back, savoring and loving. It's in the languid lulls that my heart feels full enough to burst. It's in the frenetic neediness that flares in Declan's eyes that I wonder how I ever lived without him. It's in the piercing echo as we shout each other's names that I know I can't let him go when the year is over.

I want Declan Yaeger more than anything in the world. I need him. Cherish him. Love him beyond reason.

"What are you thinking about?" His question is a quiet whisper.

"After this year…"

"Hey." His hand laces through my hair and he gently turns my face upward, until our gazes lock. The longing in his, the concern, the trust kills me. "You tell me when you're ready, Vivi. I'm not going anywhere, baby."

"Me neither, Dec. That's what I'm trying to tell you. After this year, I'm not going anywhere either. Our marriage, me and you, it's for real."

Pure love shines in his eyes, and he kisses the tip of my nose. "It's for always, Genevieve. Thank you for giving us another chance."

"Thank you for fighting for us."

Declan wraps me tighter in his arms and runs his fingers through my hair, over and over, until sleep descends over me. I let its gentle pull tug me over the edge and fall asleep clinging to the man who gave me his heart while allowing me to give mine in my own time. On my own terms.

And that makes me fall even deeper in love with him.

"GIVE US DETAILS," Abbi demands, banging her hands on the top of Indy's kitchen table.

"I thought we were here to talk about the women's shelter," I say, glancing around the little group: Indy, Abbi, Chloe, and me. Claire had a meeting with the lead singer of *The Burnt Clovers*, Derek Reiner, whose stardom has grown into an international phenomenon and Bella is at home, caring for an under-the-weather Milly.

"We'll get to that," Chloe assures me, her smile wide.

"It was a perfect weekend." I tip my head toward Chloe. "Thanks for helping with the arrangements."

"Oh." She flicks her wrist. "It was all Yaeger. Seriously, I've never seen a man so committed to planning the perfect date before. You'd think he was trying to woo you and you guys are already married."

The girls laugh and I grin. "It was very special," I agree.

"That's all you're giving us?" Abbi grumbles.

I wrinkle my nose at her. "Do you want me to make you jealous?"

"Ahh." Indy dances in her seat, pointing at Abbi. "She got you there, Abs."

Abbi sticks her tongue out at me, but her eyes are laughing. "I'm happy you had such a great time, Vivi. Honestly, I'm just jelly as fuck because Luca's been all in his head about the play-offs."

"I know what you mean," Indy agrees. "I'll be ten minutes into a story, and I look at Noah and he's staring off into space. When I call his name he's all, 'Huh? What'd you say?'"

"It's a stressful time for them," Chloe says slowly. As the Captain's girl, I think she's more conscious of the things that fall out of her mouth, especially when it comes to the team. "Especially since they won the Cup last year."

"Yeah," Indy agrees. She turns toward me. "Which is why we are all happy that you and Yaeger had this honeymoon getaway. You probably won't see him for the next few weeks."

My expression slips as her words douse me in reality. I've gotten used to my life in Boston, with Declan. Sure, the season has dictated a lot of his time but since my schedule is flexible,

I work it around his. We still spend heaps of time together. Glancing at the other girls, I realize what a luxury that is.

"Don't worry." Chloe places her hand over mine. "It's only for two months, max. And you'll have us."

"And work." Indy points at my binder, the reason we all gathered today.

"I know," I say, because I do know. Hockey is Declan's career and I want the Hawks to win the Cup as much as any of the women sitting with me. I just need to mentally adjust to the change that is coming. I open my binder. "I met with the director of Maybelle's House last week. At the moment, given the play-offs, my move to Boston, and our marriage being so...new, I think my time and resources are best utilized by supporting their current programs. I still want to open a shelter in the city, but I'm no longer on the fast track like when I first arrived."

Abbi frowns. "What changed?"

I sigh, my fingers sifting through the pages of my notes. "A few things," I admit slowly. "First, my marriage shifted a lot of my priorities. Not forever, just...for now. As I find my footing and learn to navigate all of these life changes." I don't add that it's not just my marriage, but my feelings for Declan. Over the past few weeks, they've intensified to the point where I want to be able to spend the free time he has with him. I know on some level it's foolish to put my own projects on the back burner, especially for his career. But it doesn't feel foolish. It feels like the right decision to ensure that our relationship continues to grow. Plus, it gives me the opportunity to learn about Boston's unique needs and challenges, before I dive into something so new. I don't want to take on more than I can handle, and I don't want my relationship with Declan to suffer when I do launch the women's shelter I've dreamed about.

"That makes sense." Indy shifts in her chair across from me.

"I think so too. It just feels…wrong, you know? For so many years, I've been singular in my outlook, in my approach, to getting women's programs, a shelter, off the ground. And now, it's like I'm putting everything on hold so I can spend more time with Declan."

"That's okay," Indy says. "Trust me, when Noah and I started off, I was committed to not compromising any aspect of my career for his. It's one of the reasons why I resisted a real relationship with him for so long. But then I got pregnant with Emmy and while I was still dedicated to my career, my perspective did change. It's not so much that you can't do it all; it's more that you can't do it all at the same time. You're not giving up on your dream, you're just realigning your priorities until it's the best time to bring your dream to fruition."

I heave a sigh, Indy's words more comforting than she knows. "Thank you, Indy."

"If you want it badly enough," Chloe adds, "you'll make it happen. But I think your new outlook is smart. Sometimes, we bite off more than we can chew and that ends up being a greater detriment to our success."

"And our happiness," Abbi adds.

"Exactly," I say, smiling at my friends. "Thank you, girls."

"Anytime." Abbi waves her hand and tips her chin toward my binder. "Now tell us how we can help what you've got going on with Maybelle's House."

At their eager expressions and genuine offers to help, I fill them in on my meeting from last week. I tell them all about the crafts marketplaces I'd like to expand and the educational and professional resources I think would be most beneficial to the women utilizing the shelter's programs.

Two hours later, I have a new plan to tackle, a new approach to guide me forward, and stronger friendships to see me through the next two months.

CHAPTER 19

DECLAN

"Morning, baby," I greet Vivi as soon as her eyes flutter open.

"Dec!" She gasps, her eyes wide. In the next blink, she launches herself into my arms. "I didn't hear you get in."

"It was late." I brush her hair back from her forehead and kiss her hard. "Missed you."

"Me too. How'd last night go?"

"We won." I grin. Beating Pittsburgh straight out in the first four games of the first round, has catapulted team morale. Austin is hell-bent on reminding us not to get too cocky, but man, winning four games in a row has us all on cloud nine.

"Yes!" Vivi tosses her arms around my neck. "So now, Los Angeles Knights."

"We're gonna crush 'em."

She chuckles. "Cocky. I like it."

"Nah." I lean over her, laying her out beneath me. "Just confident."

"Four for four will do that to ya."

I grin, unable to stop smiling now that I'm home, with two whole days in Boston before we fly out to L.A. I kiss my girl.

"This last week away felt like eternity," she mumbles against my lips.

"I know." I roll, pulling her on top of me.

She sits up on my abdomen, her hair spilling forward. Sleep lines from her pillow still mark her face and her sleep shirt falls off one shoulder, baring the top of her right breast. I zero in on it, already wanting to lift the shirt over her head.

"Missed you, Genevieve."

The corners of her mouth curl. "Yeah?" She leans down, covering my mouth with hers.

"Mm-hmm. Want me to show you?" I taunt.

Her fingers are already tucked under the hem of my shirt and she's dragging it upward, moving up onto her knees until it clears my head.

"If you insist," she says and I laugh.

But when Vivi turns bedroom eyes on me, my laughter falters. Because, man, my girl is something else. She's beautiful, she's smarter than I'll ever be, and her heart's still too damn big.

I make love to Vivi as the sun rises over the Boston Harbor. She cries out my name as the sky turns a golden pink, the same shade as Vivi's cheeks. I fist her hair, sitting up as she straddles my cock, and kiss her fiercely, knowing this morning has imprinted on my brain.

The same way Vivi has imprinted on my heart.

"BABY, YOU OKAY?" I ask later that night.

Vivi looks exhausted, her eyes dropping closed as we watch Netflix.

"Yeah." She yawns. "Just tired."

"Want to go to sleep?"

She shakes her head and drops it on my shoulder. "No. I want to spend time with you before L.A."

"I'll only be gone four days."

"Four days too many," she mumbles.

I snicker and wrap my arm around her, tucking her into my side. She curls into me like a cat, and I start another episode of a race-car documentary we're both into.

Vivi's even breathing catches my attention five minutes later. Man, she must be wiped. I wonder if it's the emotional toll of my being gone and her being on her own in Boston? Or are things ramping up with Maybelle's House? I know she put a pin in her plan to buy real estate and start a shelter this year but that doesn't mean she hasn't been working her ass off. Between Maybelle's House and the Harrison Foundation, I often wonder how Vivi still has time to kick it with me and socialize.

I carry her into our room, tucking her in. Her golden hair creates a halo around her head and her lips, soft and pillowy, part slightly. Kissing her forehead, I leave her to rest.

But back in the living room, I feel restless. I hated being away from Vivi this past week. Even though I was completely locked into beating Pittsburgh, especially since this is the first time I play in the NHL play-offs, I missed my girl. I hate that I'm bummed that she's passed out. Of course she's tired but I want to spend time with her, soak up the next forty-eight hours before I leave town again.

My phone buzzes and I pause the documentary.

SIMS

Yo, I got table service at Lantern on Tuesday night.

I roll my eyes. Is he joking? We have a game on Wednesday. Regardless, if we win or lose on Tuesday night, there's no way we should go out partying afterwards. I frown, knowing Sims will view my shutdown as a betrayal. Last season, when we were both single and bench warmers, it was easier to get into trouble. The weight of the team, of having a family, didn't fall so heavily on my shoulders. But now…

DECLAN

No way, man. I'm not heavy drinking till after we win the Cup.

SIMS

Pussy.

I sigh and throw down my phone. Sims pisses me off, but I try to rein it in. After all, he's not the one who's changed. I am. I've done a one-eighty from this time last year and the shift in my friendships reflect that. Now, I'm less inclined to hit a club with Sims than I am to watch game tape with Scotch. Panda and I play a hell of a lot less video games now that he's with Abbi and I'm with Vivi. But I don't have to explain that to Panda. The only guy on the team put out with me is Sims.

Should I try to rectify that in L.A.? Maybe grab dinner one night? If we chill, will he know it's not that I'm put off by his friendship, just that our outlooks don't gel at the moment?

I glance at the bedroom door, wondering if I should call it a night and crawl into bed beside Vivi.

Everything changed so quickly and yet, I like my life more now than I used to. I like the simplicity of it. I like the knowing that I'm coming home to my girl after a game. I like the little world we're building even though I would have thought it impossible a year, hell, even six months, ago.

Turning off the television, I leave my phone on the couch. I block out all the noise that comes with it and slide beneath the sheets next to my girl. Pulling her into my arms, I fall asleep to the sound of her breathing, and the scent of tangerines tinting my dreams.

"VIVI." I nudge her in the morning.

"Hmm?" She rolls over but her eyes stay closed.

"Baby, I think you're working too hard," I say seriously. She's slept for…fourteen hours.

"I'm tired," she murmurs.

Tired? I've already gone for a run, had a workout, and drank my morning smoothie. "I was hoping we could get breakfast together. Try a place in the West End? I'm flying out tomorrow morning," I remind her.

"Yeah," she agrees, rubbing her eyes. She sits up slowly and I frown since she looks…awful. "Okay."

"Are you even hungry?" I ask. "Maybe something light?" I place the back of my hand to her forehead. No fever. "Toast or oatmeal. We don't have to go crazy with cheese omelets and sausage or, Vivi!"

She springs off the bed with surprising agility for someone who was half dead three seconds ago. I sprint after her, rounding the bathroom door as she empties the contents of her stomach into the toilet bowl. Shit.

She moans. "Dec. I feel like shit."

"Okay. I got you." I grab a washcloth and run it under the faucet, passing it to her so she can clean her mouth. Instead, she drops her forehead to the rim of the toilet bowl, the washcloth clutched in her hand. I frown, opening my mouth to say something when she heaves again. "Oh, Genevieve." I move behind her, holding her hair as her shoulders shake and she gags. "You're okay, baby."

"Feel awful."

"You look good." I try to cheer her up.

"Shut up."

I clamp my mouth closed. When I'm sure she's finished, I

lift her up and carry her back to bed. "I'm going to get you some water. Can you try a cracker?"

She shakes her head, her eyelids heavy.

"You want to sleep?" I guess.

She nods.

"Okay, baby." I settle the duvet over her chest and kiss her cheek. "You rest. I'll be in the living room if you need anything." I hurry out to grab a water and some Advil.

"Thanks, Dec," she mutters right before she drops back into sleep.

All throughout the day, I keep checking on Vivi. She stirs occasionally, tossing her cookies once more. While some of her energy returns in the afternoon, she's back in bed by eight p.m.

"I don't want to leave you tomorrow," I lament, pacing at the foot of our bed. How the hell am I supposed to get on a plane when Vivi's like this? Is it food poisoning? A virus?

"I'll be fine," she croaks.

I give her a look and she shoots me an unconvincing smile.

"I'm calling Abbi," I say, knowing that Chloe is in New York for a meeting and Claire is flying out to Austin for *The Burnt Clovers* concert. She's trying to get some photos for their new album and Easton hasn't stopped grumbling about it.

Vivi doesn't protest, which alarms me even more, letting me know just how poorly she feels.

"Why you calling my girl?" Panda answers.

I roll my eyes. "Vivi's sick," I say.

"Shit. What's wrong?" he asks.

"I'm not sure," I admit, glancing at Genevieve who has fallen asleep. *Again.* Dammit, can I even go tomorrow? "I can't leave her like this, man. Her doctor says to give it another day before coming in."

"Yaeger, what's going on?" Panda sounds more serious than I've ever heard him.

"She's just…lethargic. Throwing up. Can't stay awake for more than an hour or keep anything down."

"Fever?"

"No."

"Shortness of breath?"

"No."

He sighs. "So, she's okay. She's like…normal sick."

"I guess," I say, annoyed by him downplaying Vivi's illness.

"Yaeger, don't even think about no-showing for another fucking game. Coach will bench you faster than—"

"Of course I'm not," I say automatically, although the thought *did* cross my mind. Not as an actual solution, just as a vague what-if. "I'm calling to see if Abbi could…check on her. While we're gone."

"Of course, dude."

"Do you want to ask Abbi first?"

He laughs. "Sure. Abs"—his voice grows muffled and then—"she'll be there tomorrow morning at six a.m."

"Six? We fly out at eight."

"Exactly. Abbi's got it covered so you can leave with a clear head. And hopefully, it's just a twenty-four-hour bug and Vivi feels better tomorrow. No need for the doctor."

I start at how casually he drops "Vivi." But I like it; the way my team calls her that. It's like she's part of our Hawks family, not just mine, and it's nice to both belong somewhere, together.

"Tell Abbi she has my unending gratitude," I say, relaxing.

"She's already concocting schemes for you, me, and Scotch to watch Emmaline for an entire weekend so the girls can shove off to Miami."

I laugh, volunteering to babysit.

"Damn, man. Why'd you have to go and be so eager about it?" Panda grumbles.

"See you tomorrow, Panda."

"Later, Yaeger."

I hang up the phone and walk aimlessly around my condo. I double-check my bag to make sure everything is packed. Having done this so many times, I could pack in my sleep, but I feel restless, unsure of what to do other than hover over Vivi and hope she feels better soon.

But when she vomits at five a.m., my hopes are dashed.

I leave for L.A. with a knot in my chest, even as Abbi's capable hands shoo me out the door.

CHAPTER 20
VIVI

Declan's been gone for two days. After speaking with my doctor on the phone, she thinks it's just viral and recommended rest. Abbi's flitted in an out of our condo like clockwork, bringing food, ginger ale, magazines, and random bits of chitchat. She goes out of her way to make sure I'm okay and while I have moments where I don't feel like death, by day three of feeling off, I'm starting to get worried and put another call in for Dr. Shams.

Laying in bed, watching old movies on Lifetime, it's a commercial that finally clues me in. A tampon commercial. While I watch the woman cringe onscreen and pull a tampon from her purse, apprehension explodes in the pit of my stomach as panic makes my mind race.

Holy shit. When was the last time I had a period? I've been on the shot for so long and…fuck, when was my last shot? I jump from the bed, ignoring the protest in my stomach, and swipe up my phone. Navigating to the calendar, I swipe left, going back four months until I see the appointment I had with Dr. Collins, in Nashville.

Horror washes over me. I was supposed to go for my shot six weeks ago. And I didn't. To be honest, I forgot all about it.

And then… Declan wooed me in Oak Bluffs, and I cheekily laughed off the use of a condom and now…

I could be pregnant. With Declan's baby. Again.

My hands shake as I stumble to the bathroom, spewing vomit just short of the toilet bowl. Dread fills my body with dead weight, and I drop to my knees, resting my cheek against the cool tile of the bathroom floor.

The smell is revolting but I don't care. I don't have the energy to move. I don't have the wherewithal to do anything except…panic.

Will Declan be happy? Will he want this, a baby, with me, right now?

And oh, God, what if we lose it? What if I lose our baby again?

My hand spreads wide over my abdomen, remembering with acute clarity the painful ordeal I experienced the last time I was pregnant. Will that happen again? Tears fill my eyes, spilling over and dropping to the floor.

I am a pathetic mess. I need to get up and…move.

My phone rings and I swear, groping for it as if it would be on the bathroom floor.

Groaning, I stagger to my feet. My nostrils flare and my lips curl, another wave of nausea hitting me, as I take in the vomit I need to clean up. I plug my nose and gather the necessary cleaning supplies, making sure the bathroom bears no trace of my mishap before Abbi arrives.

When I pick up my phone, I see the missed call from Dr. Shams and wince. When I call her back and explain that I think I'm pregnant, she tosses around words like hyperemesis gravidarum, IV fluids, hospital, a blood test, and doxylamine. By the time I hang up, with an appointment for tomorrow, I'm dizzy.

My phone beeps again.

HENRY

You knocked up yet?

His message would be funny if I wasn't already panicking. But right now, I couldn't be more grateful than to read his name, his message, and know that I can confide in him.

But first, a test.

I could call Abbi and ask her to bring me one. But I haven't known her that long and it feels wrong, confiding in someone Declan knows about a possible pregnancy, before telling him. My stomach roils and I know there's no way in hell I'll make it to a pharmacy on my own.

So, I do that sensible thing. I pull up Instacart and order a delivery. Three pregnancy tests, peach sparkling water, and pretzels.

It arrives outside our condo door an hour later. Too embarrassed to meet the courier's eyes, I mutter my thanks, and race back to the bathroom.

The longest three minutes of my life pass and then—

Holy shit. I'm pregnant. Declan and I are pregnant!

Tears stream down my cheeks and my fingers tremble as I set the test down next to the bathroom sink. I wash my hands and plop back down on the closed toilet bowl. Should I call Declan? No, he has a game in—I glance at the time on my phone—forty minutes.

My phone chimes and I jump, relieved when I read Abbi's message.

ABBI

Hey babe, something came up at work so I'll be later with dinner. You okay?

VIVI

Yes! Feeling better. Don't even worry about dinner. I'm good. You have been a lifesaver and I can't thank you for all your help this week.

ABBI

Stop, was nothing. You sure you're good?

VIVI

Positive.

I flinch and then laugh at the word.

VIVI

I'm fine. Talk soon.

ABBI

OK. XX

Except, I am so not fine. Not even a little.

I scroll through my contacts and find Henry's name.

"Viv, I miss your voice," he answers.

"Henry," I sound panicked.

He detects it immediately. "What's wrong? You okay?"

"I'm…pregnant. I'm fucking pregnant," I blurt out.

"Okay," he says slowly. Then, because he knows me so well, "Breathe, Viv. Just breathe." He starts inhaling and exhaling slowly through the line and I snort, but after a few moments of box breathing, I do feel better. "This is…good news, isn't it?"

"I don't know," I admit, trying to take stock of how I feel. "Since the moment I found out, all I can think of is how Dec will react."

"Dec," he repeats. "Cute."

"Focus!"

"Sorry. Okay, so you haven't told him yet?"

"He's about to take the ice against L.A."

"Right. And you're freaking out?"

"Completely."

"Viv," Henry's tone is soft. "He's going to be over the fucking moon. I've never seen a man look at a woman the way Declan looks at you."

"Mac looks at you the same way."

"True," he chuckles. "But what you and Declan have, it's real, Viv. You need to have faith in your relationship, in your history, and tell him."

"Yeah." I take a deep breath. "You're right."

"Of course I'm right."

"Should I tell him tonight? Or wait until he's back from L.A.?" The questions feel like déjà vu and for some reason, that worries me. It leaves me feeling hesitant and unable to make a decision.

"Whenever you think the time is right," Henry says, and I can hear the question he doesn't ask. *Why are you so worried about this?*

"Okay," I say with more confidence than I feel.

"You got this, Viv."

"Right."

"Hey," his tone softens. "Congratulations, Mama."

I smile, pressing my fingertips to my lips. "Thank you, Henry."

"Call me if you need anything."

"I will. Love you."

"Me too. 'Bye, baby girl."

I hang up the phone and go back to bed. Lying down, I stare at the ceiling. My thoughts trip over themselves, some worried, some exuberant, some terrified. I watch Declan's game in bed, managing to eat a few pretzels. I cheer when they win, knowing he'll be in a great mood tonight.

I settle back against the pillows and wait for him to call. But then I need to throw up again and disappointment twists my stomach when I realize that in the ten minutes I was immobile on the bathroom floor, I missed Dec's call.

Irrational tears flood my eyes and I swipe at them, annoyed by their presence. Annoyed with myself...and with Declan for not calling again.

I try him back, but it goes to voicemail. A few minutes later, a message comes through.

DECLAN

> Hi, Vivi love. How are you feeling? Do you need anything? Sorry I missed you. Service in here is spotty. I'm kicking it with Sims for a bit. Haven't hung out in forever. But I'll check in with you tonight. Love you, babe.

I frown at his message, my stomach dipping. Why can't he step out, into cellular service, and call me? Sighing, I close my eyes and wait for him to call.

Except when he does, I'm in the bathroom throwing up. Again. And when I try him back, I get his voicemail. Again.

I stare at my phone angrily, beyond upset that I can't get in touch with Declan. As my anger fades into fatigue, I fall asleep with my phone clutched against my chest, so I won't miss any more of Declan's calls. Except he doesn't call again.

And when I wake in the morning and read my messages, I know why.

AUSTIN MERRICK

> Genevieve, call me when you get this.
> Yaeger's been arrested.

INDY

> Hey, are you okay? Can I come by?

NOAH SCOTCH

> Yaeger and Sims are being held overnight.
> As of now, they're not charged with anything.

CHLOE

> There was a drug bust at a club! Can you believe that? I'm sure Yaeger and Sims weren't involved.

ABBI

How are you feeling? Don't panic. I'm sure there's an explanation.

LUCA PANDATELLI

Vivi, give me a call. Let me know where your head's at.

And then, the newsworthy headline.

Boston Hawks players Eddie Sims and Declan Yaeger Spotted Partying at Lantern. Strippers, Drugs, and Arrests Ensue.

My heart races and my head throbs. The wave of nausea that overtakes me is partly from pregnancy and partly from panic. I sprint to the bathroom, making it just in time. Heaving over the toilet bowl, sweat beads along my hairline.

I pull myself up on shaky legs and move to pee. Except when I pull down my underwear I see the drops of blood. Bright red. Fuck. Oh, no, this isn't happening. Fear mixes with my nausea and I start to shake as my mind spins.

I must be having an out-of-body experience. I must be imagining this. It must be a hellish nightmare, right? This can't be happening *again.*

Oh, Dec, I need you. I can't do this again. Not by myself.

My phone rings and hope swells in my chest. Except when I swipe it up, Declan's name isn't on the screen.

"Henry."

He sighs heavily. "You okay, baby girl?"

"No."

"I know. I saw the headlines, and I'm sure you're freaking out. But there's more to the story than we know from a gossip magazine or Twitter. There always is."

"He's on Twitter?" I gasp.

"Trending."

"Fuck, Henry. I'm spotting."

"What?" Alarm rings in my best friend's tone. "Shit, okay. What do you need?"

"I don't know. I can't even think. Henry, I'm spotting and I'm sick. I'm so fucking sick," I cry out as my stomach roils. "Declan's not here. And I need him. I don't know what to do," I sob. "Henry, what should I do?"

"Okay, Viv, you shouldn't be alone. I'm going to book a flight."

I close my eyes, trying to hold back my tears. I suddenly want to be as far away from here as possible. I don't want to be in Boston and its unfamiliar city streets. I want my home. The Willow Tree. Granddaddy.

But when I stand, a gush of blood rushes between my thighs, staining them red. My stomach twists painfully and I cry out again.

"Viv, listen to me," Henry's voice is frantic. In the background, I hear him calling for Mac.

"I'm bleeding, Henry. Not spotting. Bleeding." I grip the vanity for balance as my head spins.

"Mac and I are coming to you. Stay right where you are, baby girl. I'm calling 9-1-1."

"What? No!" I protest, but blood is running down my legs, forming a puddle on the floor. "Oh, fuck. There's too much blood. I'm losing the baby." I grab a towel and sit on it, at a loss for what to do next. I drop my head into my hand and sob. Tears pour from my eyes as blood rushes out of me. "Henry, I can't do this again. Not without him."

"Mac called 9-1-1. There's an ambulance on the way. Give me your friend's number—Abbi? Give me a number, Genevieve."

There's so much blood. The towel is soaked through. Coldness sweeps up my skin and my head grows dizzy. Fuzzy. I glance at my phone but the words on the screen run together. Nothing makes sense.

Nothing.

"Genevieve, are you there?"

I'm here. I open my mouth, but no words come out. Instead, the floor rushes to meet my face and I go down hard.

CHAPTER 21
DECLAN

"Yaeger, I'm fucking sorry, all right?"

I glare at Sims as we're released from goddamn jail. The officer hands me a small plastic bag, my busted phone inside.

"It was a misunderstanding," Sims pleads as I stride out of the place.

Fucking Sims and his stupid ass got us mixed up in a drug bust that went down last night at Lantern. While cops raided the upper area of the club, packed with connected guys, strippers, blow, and so much cash, my friend was getting his dick sucked by a girl slurring so badly, she probably didn't know her own name.

Dragging his sorry ass out of there was the plan. After a big win, a steak dinner and a beer, I headed back to the hotel, intent on talking with Vivi. But each time I called her, she didn't answer. Then I ran into East and Panda and decided to kick it with them for a bit. An hour later, I had a stream of drunken texts from Sims and knew I had to pull him from the club he was partying at before he become a team liability. At the urging of our shared agent, Callie, I swung by Lantern, located him, and ended the night in fucking handcuffs.

Now, I'm a married man with my eyes set on the Cup and I'm leaving jail. Luckily, Callie and my lawyer were able to clear everything up and although Sims and I were held for the night, there aren't any charges against us. Especially since the girl sucking Sims off wasn't part of the prostitution ring and thank fuck, was legal.

"What're you, not going to talk to me?" Sims doesn't know when to quit.

I whirl around, just before we leave the jail. "Sims, you got our asses arrested. Do you know how fucking lucky we are that things played out the way they did? That we're not being charged with fucking drug possession?"

"We didn't possess any drugs," he reminds me slowly, like I'm the one that needs a goddamn life lesson.

I throw my hands in the air. "We're playing in the NHL play-offs, Sims. The play-offs. The last thing you should be doing is hitting a club and drinking your face off just to get some woman whose name you don't know to put your dick in her mouth."

He sputters, laughter lightening his eyes. I resist the urge to cock back my arm and let it fly at his face. Why doesn't he care about the team right now? About our names? Our reputations?

I tug the back of my head. "I gotta call Vivi."

"Married life ruined you," my friend accuses.

I glare at him, holding back the ugly words that rattle inside my head, and push through the doors.

Callie and Austin wait on the front steps, their arms crossed, their expressions stamped in anger.

Austin points at me. "You were at the wrong place at the wrong time." He points at Sims. "You're a goddamn liability. Let's go." He turns around and we follow him, like scolded teenagers trailing after our dad.

While a year ago, I could have easily been mixed up with Sims and the trouble he found himself in, now, I'm not about that life. I don't want to hit the clubs, drink my face off, and screw around with random women. I want my Vivi who must be worried sick and furious as fuck.

Callie's already fielding phone calls, trying to keep a consistent message on this nightmare as it spins in news outlets. The theme seems to be wrong place, wrong time, which I'll gladly cling to.

Once we get into the black Suburban with tinted windows, Sims sulks, sliding down in his seat and glancing out the window. Callie rides up front while Austin moves to the third row. I plop down across the aisle from Sims, so angry I could snap. I'm tired, sore, and desperate to talk to Vivi. Knowing we still have a game to play tonight, I need to clear my head. I need to get my mind right. In order to do that, I need Vivi.

I hold out my hand. "Cap, my phone is busted. Can I call Vivi?"

Austin shoots me a sympathetic look. "Sure."

I dial her number and hold the phone to my ear, frowning when it goes straight to voicemail. "Has anyone talked to her? She's been sick. For her phone to be off…"

Austin shrugs. "We've been trying her. Me, a couple of the guys, the girls. No one's been able to get through. Abbi went over there an hour ago."

"And?" I ask, panic starting to rise in my chest. Out of the corner of my eye, I see Sims turn to look at me.

"She didn't answer," Austin says quietly.

Callie ends her phone call. "I called your super, had him check your place. Hope you don't mind."

I shake my head, waiting.

Callie turns in her seat and looks right at me. "She wasn't there, Yaeger, but—"

"What the hell does that mean?" I explode, the anger I kept simmering just under the surface finding an outlet.

Callie looks startled and I instantly feel badly for yelling at her.

"Sorry." I look away. "I just, I'm worried."

"I know," she says. "I know you are. And you should be."

Sims freezes beside me, and Austin swears.

"There was a lot of blood, Yaeger. The super just called me back and Genevieve was taken to Mass General a few hours ago."

I feel the blood drain from my face, my body, as I try to make sense of Callie's words. "Mass General? Is she okay? What the fuck happened? What blood?"

"I don't know. I called the hospital, and they won't give me any information but—"

"I'm on it," I cut her off, Googling Mass General for the phone number. The second it appears on screen, I press it.

Silence falls over the SUV as everyone holds their breath, waiting. When I finally connect with a human and not a damn automation service, I'm so on edge, I feel ready to snap.

"My name is Declan Yaeger. My wife, Genevieve, was taken by ambulance a few hours ago and I need to know if she's okay. Is she okay? What the fuck happened?" I blurt out. And then, "Sorry for swearing."

"It's all right," the woman on the other line says. "Let's see if we can help you, Mr. Yaeger. Your wife's name, Genevieve—"

"Kelley," I supply. "She hasn't legally changed her name yet."

"Correct," the woman says. "Okay." I hear her fingers clacking on a keyboard and then, "I'm so sorry, Mr. Yaeger, but I'm unable to give an update over the phone."

I pull the cell away from my ear and glare at it, as if that will help answer what the fuck is going on. "My wife—"

"I know. And I'm sorry, sir. But there is a number here for you to call. A Mr. Henry Stevens—"

"Henry's there?"

"Let me give you his number." She rattles off the number and I repeat it aloud as Callie punches it into her phone. The second I disconnect, Callie is passing me her cell.

"It's ringing," she says.

I nod.

"Hello?" a man answers.

"Henry? It's Declan."

"Oh, thank God. Hi, Declan, this is Mac."

Mac? Who the fuck is Mac? I'm about to ask when—

"Declan? It's Henry. Listen, Viv's okay."

I breathe out a sigh of relief. My body sags forward as gratitude I've never known sweeps through me. Tears fill my eyes as I hang my head, ignoring everyone in the SUV.

"What the hell happened, Henry?" I bite out, desperate for answers.

"Genevieve's okay," he repeats. "I just talked to her—"

"What the fuck happened? Why was there blood? Did someone hurt her, did she—"

"She's pregnant."

I slam back into the SUV seat and glare at the ceiling. My girl, *my wife*, is pregnant and I'm here, fresh out of jail, in fucking L.A.? Panic races through me as I realize what Henry's saying. "Is the baby—"

"We don't know," he cuts me off, saving me from having to ask the question.

Sims swears beside me, and Callie's expression turns sympathetic. I feel Austin's hand land on my shoulder, and I don't shake it off. Right now, I need someone to ground me to this moment before I fly off the handle and knock Sims's teeth down his throat.

"Can I talk to her?" I ask Henry.

He sighs, "Listen, Declan. She's sleeping. She's... struggling."

"I'm coming home."

"I know. But you have a game tonight."

"Fuck that," I bite out.

"She wants you to play," Henry says, confusing me. There's no way in hell Vivi would want me to take the ice tonight knowing that she's laid up in the hospital, dealing with a potential miscarriage like all those years ago.

"I promised her I'd step up, be there for her," I continue.

"If you don't play tonight, your career is over," he reminds me and I realize just how much Vivi confides in him.

"I don't care." I truly don't. Nothing is more important than Vivi. And our baby.

"She does," Henry states. "She doesn't want you to resent her."

"I'd never—"

"She can't handle it, man. Listen to me. Suit up and get on the ice. Play, win the game. Give it everything you have. And then come home. Be with her. Love her and show her that you've got her back, but not at the expense of everything y'all just built. You know why she didn't tell you she was pregnant that summer?"

"Because she didn't want me to give up my dream," I say, feeling sick as the words form in my mouth.

"She still doesn't, Declan."

I pinch the top of my nose, feeling the tears as they trickle over my fingers. "I need to be with her, man."

"I know. I'll stay with her until you get here. Don't worry, she's in good hands. The doctor said the next twenty-four hours will be touch and go. Play the game, let her see you on that screen, and then come home. She'll be here."

"Henry," I sob, choking up.

"I know, Declan. Can I call this number if I need to reach you?"

"Yeah, it's my agent, Callie's number. She'll be at the game." I glance at Callie who nods to confirm.

"Good luck tonight. Make our girl proud." Henry disconnects.

"Fuck." I pass Callie back her phone.

She takes it and gives me a look filled with such compassion that I have to look away. Because her understanding guts me. Makes me feel so fucking guilty for being here, while Vivi's in Boston, without me, hurting. Again.

"I know you've got a lot going on. I know this fucking sucks," Austin says quietly.

"But we have a game tonight," I finish the thought aloud so he doesn't have to.

He squeezes my shoulder again before removing his hand.

"Look, I'm sorry, man," Sims says next to me.

I nod, but I don't look at them. I keep my gaze trained out the window, wondering how Vivi is, and if our marriage can survive whatever the hell comes next.

I PLAY IN A FOG. For the first time in my life, I'm incapable of getting into the right headspace.

I miss easy blocks, I'm slow to react, and for two long periods, I struggle. Thank God my team knows when to step up because Panda plays superior in goal. Easton is on fire, scoring three goals and having two assists in the first two periods alone.

But in the third period, everything goes to shit. And I mean everything. We're up by one goal when Noah hits the ice. He collides with the Knights defenseman and goes down, calling out in agony while gripping his left knee. Silence descends over the arena. Even the cocky L.A. fans don't say shit.

I hold my breath, feeling the nausea that has been roiling in my stomach since I spoke with Henry rise into my throat. *Get up, Scotch.*

He doesn't. He's taken off the ice, a dazed expression on his face. The game resumes with Sims being called up. By the tightness in Austin's jaw and the constant muttering by Coach, I can tell no one is particularly happy with this development.

Sims has the Boston Hawks name in everyone's mouth and it sure as fuck isn't positive. Now, it's like his bad behavior is being rewarded. My hands curl into fists as he skates onto the ice and I turn away.

Even though he plays hard, our team is too out of sync. The remaining six minutes pass by with agonizing slowness. It's like we're all moving in slow motion, our senses dulled, our motions sloppy. L.A. scores twice, overtaking our lead, and we lose by one point when the buzzer sounds.

Team morale is at an all time low, but I don't give a shit. I just want to get the fuck out of L.A. and back to Genevieve. It sinks even lower when we learn that Scotch's knee injury is going to require surgery, effectively ending his play for the rest of the season.

I swear and pull out the new phone Callie replaced for me. Nothing from Vivi. Nothing from Henry. Last I checked in, the doctor had given Vivi something for her nausea and she had fallen back to sleep.

Now that the game is over, I can allow my panic to consume me. And it's not just panic over her well-being, even though I'm worried about her health. It's panic for the baby. It's panic over the fact that if we lose this baby, Genevieve may never recover. With such a complicated history and a rocky start to our marriage, do I even have a shot with my wife at this point?

I go through the motions of checking out of the hotel and heading to the airport. I've never been more relieved to land back in Boston. I blow off the team bus to pick up my car from the arena and catch an Uber straight to the hospital.

Plowing through the front doors, I run straight to reception. Before I can shout my questions at the woman behind the desk, my name is called.

I spin around, nearly colliding with the guy before me.

"Declan, I'm Mac," he says, taking my arm and pulling me toward the elevators. "Genevieve's in room 1248."

"Who the hell are you, man?" I ask as I let him usher me into the elevator.

"Henry's boyfriend," he explains like it's obvious.

"Oh. Oh, shit." I swipe my fingers across my forehead, feeling like a giant douchebag. All those years I thought Henry and Genevieve were together, all that time I spent jealous of her best friend and…Henry is gay? "How the hell did I not know this?"

Mac chuckles and shakes his head. "I have no idea. Viv says you're pretty oblivious." He shrugs and I laugh.

"How is she?"

"Hanging in there. They're going to do a blood test in the morning and then again, forty-eight hours later to check her HCG levels. Then, we'll know more about the viability of her pregnancy."

I look at him like he's speaking another language. He kind of is. "What the hell's an HCG?"

Mac gives me a pitying look. "Okay, so…" he walks me through the pregnancy hormone and how it begins to double. His explanation is very thorough and then he adds, "For right now, the doctor is treating her nausea from her hyperemesis gravidarum."

I groan. "What the fuck, man?"

He shakes his head. "I'll let the doctor bring you up to speed."

Then, we're outside the hospital room door and I'm pushing in, careful to be quiet as Henry jumps to his feet, his finger pressed to his lips.

Vivi is sleeping. My sweet girl is fast asleep, her hair splayed across the pillow, her body wrapped in a hospital gown. She looks so fragile and weak, so exhausted with purple half moons underneath her eyes. Relief that she's okay rushes through me but it's quickly washed away by guilt. She needed me and I wasn't here for her. Not the way I promised her I would be.

Can she forgive me? If we lose this baby, will she ever forgive me?

CHAPTER 22
VIVI

"Hey, baby girl." Mac brushes a kiss over the top of my head, as my eyes slowly open. The sterile hospital room comes into focus, and I turn until I meet Mac's gaze. "How are you feeling?"

"Like shit," I admit.

He makes a sympathetic cluck, his hand reaching out for my arm. "You're going to be okay, Viv. You're the most badass chick I know."

"Thanks, Mac."

He tilts his head toward the hallway where I can picture Henry, pacing back and forth, demanding answers from doctors. I hear the muffled sounds of a man's voice and shake my head. "He's worried about you," Mac says.

"I didn't mean to worry y'all." Tears sting my eyes and I blink furiously, hating how emotionally unbalanced I feel. All I want to do is cry. And sleep.

"Not Henry, although he's worried about you too."

My eyebrows bend together as I wait for Mac to explain.

"Declan," he says softly.

"He's here?" Hope fills my chest and I relax against the pillow. Declan's here. He came back...for me.

"Hasn't left your side in hours. Just now"—Mac nods toward the door—"when the doctor showed up. I think Declan scares him."

I chuckle.

"And Henry went to get you 'some edible food options,'" he explains in air quotes, causing me to grin.

"Y'all are too good to me."

"Nah." Mac shakes his head. "We just love you."

"Love y'all too. And I'm real happy that Henry found you. He tell his dad yet?"

Mac nods. "Mr. Stevens is coming around. Slowly."

Genuine happiness for my friend makes me smile. "I'm happy to hear it, Mac."

Exhaustion weighs my limbs down and my eyes close. My hands rest on my abdomen. I'm quiet for a long minute, Declan's muffled voice outside my hospital door. But, I'd rather ask Mac than Dec, so I force myself to say, "And the baby?"

"No update yet," Mac murmurs and my eyes open. "But you're going to pull through this, Viv. No matter the outcome, you and Declan will make it through. That man loves you something fierce."

I work a swallow, nodding. I love him too. But is love enough when the loss is so great? Can we move on from this experience after we barely came to terms with the last one? I brush my fingers over my stomach. God, please don't let me lose this baby. I pray to God and then I pray to Saint Genevieve. I pray and I bargain and I hope.

The door to my hospital room opens. "How many times has she thrown up?" the doctor asks.

"Too many," Declan answers and then, he looks at me, sees that I'm awake, and rushes over, dropping to his knees. The most heartbreaking expression, fear and hope and love, crosses his face. "Vivi, God, baby." He takes my fingers in his and drops his forehead to the back of my hand. My hand grips his hair as he murmurs, "I've been so worried. So fucking scared. Vivi, are you okay?" He looks up, his lips grazing my thumb.

Now that he's here, with me, I sink into the strength he provides. It's a relief, really, to not have to hold it all together. Instead, I let my tears fall and I shift toward him, letting him witness the crushing heartache I feel.

Declan moves faster than lightning, perching on the edge of my bed and gathering me in his arms. "Shh, baby, it's okay. You're okay. I'm here and I got you. No matter what, Vivi, we'll be okay," he murmurs, over and over, pressing kisses into my hair.

The doctor clears his throat and Declan shoots him a dirty look.

"Genevieve, how are you feeling?" Dr. Scotts asks.

I manage to pull myself together enough to meet his gaze. "A little better," I admit.

"Good. According to the ultrasound, the bleeding was caused by a subchorionic hematoma," Dr. Scotts says. "It can be common in early pregnancy and can cause bleeding."

"Even as much as I had?" I ask, doubtful.

"Yes," he says, making me feel a tiny bit better. Restoring a glimmer of hope.

Declan squeezes my hand and his arm around my shoulders tightens.

"The nurses are going to keep your fluids IV going and we'll monitor your hyperemesis gravidarum. We'll keep you for another two days, just to make sure your levels are okay. Then, we'll do another HCG test and you can go home. Just stay off your feet and get as much rest as you can while we wait the next few days out."

"Okay," I murmur.

"I've already brought your husband up to speed, but do you have any questions?" Dr. Scotts asks.

"No. Thank you, Dr. Scotts."

He opens the door just as Henry appears, takeout bags clutched in both his hands. Dr. Scotts mutters under his breath but leaves the room and Mac chortles. "What'd you do? Raid a convenience store?"

Henry laughs and places the bags down. "I didn't know what Viv was in the mood for."

"Are you hungry? Thirsty?" Declan asks me.

"No, I'm okay for now." I point at all the takeout containers Henry and Mac unload. "You guys eat."

"I see you met Mac," Henry says to Declan.

"Yeah, what the hell, man. Why didn't you tell me you're gay?" Declan uncaps a bottle of water and hands it to me.

I take a tentative sip, watching this entertaining moment play out.

Henry shrugs. "Does it matter?"

"Fuck no," Declan laughs. "But I wouldn't have asked you if you've got a roommate."

At that, Henry cracks up and Declan and Mac join in.

"Thanks for taking care of Vivi." Declan holds out his hand to both guys to shake.

I roll my eyes. Men.

Once my three favorite guys have plates of food, I look at Declan and ask, "What happened in L.A.?"

Declan heaves out a breath. "I know you're not going to believe me—"

"You don't know that," I say.

He gulps. "I swear to you, it was wrong place, wrong time. I went out to dinner with Sims, we had a steak and a beer. Then, I went back to the hotel, met up with the Easton and Panda, and hung out for a little bit. Sims went to a club downtown, Lantern. He kept messaging me and each text was worse than the last. He was drunk off his ass, we had another game the following night, so I went to pick him up. When I found him"—Dec pauses, wincing—"well, he wasn't in a respectable way. A few minutes later, the police raided the place and took us all in. Sims and I were cleared, no charges, but they held us for the night until everything got sorted. I've been going out of my mind worried about you. Austin told me no one could get in touch with you. And then Callie, my agent, got in touch with the super. Fuck, baby, I was dying when they told me about the blood and the ambulance. The hospital wouldn't give out info over the phone…" He looks at Henry. "Smart thinking, leaving your number. Thanks, man."

"That was all Mac," Henry says.

Declan thanks him.

I roll my lips together and study Declan. He looks awful, pretty much as bad as I feel. His eyes are bloodshot, his clothes are wrinkled, and his hair looks like he's been pulling at it for the last day, all haphazard curls. My poor guy. I can't imagine how shitty the past two days were but I'm so happy he's here. "Declan—"

"I'm so fucking sorry, Vivi. I never meant to let you down. Or our baby." He takes my hand, shaking his head. "Whatever you need from me, I'm in. I swear to you, I won't fuck this up again. It was all a stupid mistake. I didn't want to leave Sims like that, wide open to start a PR nightmare for the Hawks, right when we're in the play-offs. And then, I made it a million times worse by getting arrested. And not being here for you, when you're sick. And hurting. I'll never forgive myself, Vivi."

"Stop," I say, knowing I need to shut this down. Henry tilts his head toward the hallway and he and Mac quietly excuse themselves. I shift in the hospital bed and reach for Declan's hand. "Dec, I don't blame you."

"But I wasn't here. You needed me and—"

"You were doing your job. You were living your dream. That's what I've always wanted for you."

Grief slashes across his face as he shakes his head. "Genevieve, knowing you were in the hospital, potentially miscarrying our baby, and I had to skate onto the fucking ice was one of the worst moments of my life. I can't imagine how bad it was for you, being by yourself, being put in an ambulance, and…" He pauses, his voice cracking. "I'm so sorry."

"No," I tell him, squeezing his hand. "As scared as I was when I saw the blood, as much as I wanted you with me, I never blamed you for not being here. Never. I wanted you to play the game. I wanted to watch you win."

He snorts.

"And then, I wanted you to come home to me. I'm scared, Dec."

"I am too," he admits, dropping his forehead to mine. "But we'll be okay, Vivi. No matter what."

"No matter what," I agree, breathing in his exhales. Tears well in my eyes and Declan's brow furrows. He clasps the side of my face, his thumb stroking my cheek.

"I love you, Genevieve. I want to make a family with you. And God, I hope this is the start of that, but if this doesn't go the way we want it to, we'll still have each other. Promise me we can get through this."

I pull back so I can look into his eyes and give him the reassurance he's been searching for since the day he made me his wife. "We can get through anything, Declan. And we will."

His eyes fill with tears as mine fall and he grips the back of my head, kissing me hard.

DECLAN STAYS with me at the hospital while Henry and Mac return to our condo. The following night, I force Declan to attend his hockey game and Henry and Mac join me with popcorn while we cheer him on.

After three long days in the hospital, I'm discharged with a prescription for doxylamine. Declan takes me home, where we'll wait for news of my blood test. Henry and Mac have cleaned our condo and stocked my nightstand with gossip magazines and books before flying back to Nashville.

"They're good friends," Declan says when he takes in the state of our apartment. "They really didn't have to do all of this."

"They're the best," I agree.

"Want some tea?" Dec asks as he tucks me in.

"Only if you have some with me."

He kisses the tip of my nose and agrees, as his phone rings. "What do you want?" he answers.

I frown.

Dec snorts, then he passes me the phone.

"Who is it?" I mouth.

"It's Sims. He wants to talk to you."

I give Declan a confused look, but he shrugs.

I take the phone and bring it to my hear. "Hello?"

"Genevieve, I am so fucking sorry," Sims, a guy I've barely spoken to, blurts out.

I laugh, surprised more than anything.

"No. I'm serious. I've been shitty to you from the moment I met you because…well, I was jealous."

"Jealous?"

"You took my wingman," he explains, his tone playful.

"Ohhh," I say, understanding the source of his indifference now.

"I was shitty. I'm sorry."

"It's okay."

"No, it's not. But it's nice of you to pretend otherwise."

I grin, liking Sims's honesty. He's refreshing.

"The other night was my fault. One-hundred percent my selfish, drunk-ass fault," he says.

"I know; Dec told me."

"Damn. He sold me out that fast?" Sims asks.

I laugh again and Declan lifts his eyebrows in surprise.

"I'm sorry if I made you worry. If I caused you any stress. I'm so fucking sorry to hear you were in the hospital," Sims says sincerely.

"It's okay."

"I just wanted to make sure that you're okay. You, Genevieve, and you and Yaeger... Geneger. Yaevi. I'll have to work on your couple name."

"Oh, God." I gasp, laughing in earnest now. "Neither of those options, please."

"It's still a work in progress, Genevieve. Give me some time."

"Take all the time you need."

He chuckles. "You sure you're okay?"

"Yeah, we're just...waiting for an update about the baby."

"I'm sending all my good thoughts and energy your way. Hell, I'm even going to toss up a prayer."

"I appreciate that."

"If you want to know anything about L.A. or lockup..."

"No. No, I'm good." I look at Declan. "I trust Dec."

"I'm happy to hear it."

"But, thanks for calling, Sims."

"It's nice to meet you, Genevieve."

"You too. Call me Vivi," I say.

"All right, Vivi. We'll do lunch when you're feeling up to it."

"Looking forward to it," I agree, passing the phone back to Declan.

He exchanges a few words with Sims before ending the call and placing his phone down. "He's a pain in the ass but not a completely shit friend."

"Nah, he's a good guy."

Dec's eyes narrow. "You talked to him for two seconds."

I shrug. "I'm a good judge of character."

Declan laughs. "You sure about that?" He points to himself.

I grab his index finger and twist it. "I'm sure."

His expression grows somber as he looks at me, his eyes darting down to my belly. "Let me get your tea."

"Okay." I smile.

Dec links his fingers with mine, his gaze serious. He leans forward and kisses me for a long moment. "Marry me, Vivi."

I pull back, startled. "What? We're already married."

He smiles, his eyes shining. "Marry me again. Me and you. Our vows, our way. Let's grow a family, baby."

I smile, letting the love in Dec's eyes wash over me. "You want to marry me again?"

"I'd marry you every day until we're old and wrinkly as raisins. And even then."

"Okay," I whisper. "Yes."

"Yes," he agrees, pulling me in for another kiss.

I fall headfirst into this one and don't come up for air until my phone rings.

"It's the hospital." I swipe it up.

"Answer," Declan commands.

"Hello?" I say hesitantly, crossing my fingers and toes for good news. The doctor runs me through my blood test results and I can't stop the smile that splits my face.

"What'd he say?" Declan asks as soon as I hang up.

"The numbers doubled. The baby's okay," I sob, feeling the tears fall down my cheeks. "Our baby is okay."

Declan wraps me in his arms and hugs me close, kissing my forehead. "We're all going to be okay, Genevieve. We're going to be a family."

CHAPTER 23
DECLAN

TWO MONTHS LATER

The breeze is gentle, the sunshine is warm, and the look in Vivi's eyes when she meets me under the swaying branches of the willow tree in the front yard of her childhood home is pure love.

Mac swipes a tear from under his eye. "Hey, baby girl." He hugs Genevieve.

Henry kisses Vivi's cheek and murmurs, "You look beautiful." He turns to me and holds out his hand. "Declan, you finally became a man."

I chuckle and shake his hand. "It's about time, huh?"

Henry laughs. "I gotta say I like this version of your wedding better than the first one."

"Me too," I agree.

I stare at Genevieve, letting the love and light of my girl, right here in the heart of Tennessee, wash over me. God, I am a lucky man.

I lost my way and the woman who helped me find it is the same girl who set me on my path from the beginning. Can't blaze trails without some star dust and the star in this story is definitely Genevieve Rae.

I extend my hand and she takes it, our wedding bands clinking together. But today isn't about the town, Mr. Harrison's legacy, or appearances. Today is about us, our love and commitment, and the family we're growing.

Vivi and I face each other. Her hair is plaited back from her face, a braid that wraps over the top of her head like a crown. My queen. Her eyes glimmer, filled with emotions that I feel in my soul.

"Genevieve Rae, my Vivi," I start and Mac sobs. "From the first time I kissed you—"

"You mean, when I kissed you." She smirks.

I grin. "Yes. From that moment, I knew it was you or no one. You've always been it for me. We were so young, but even then, we knew what we had was rare. Special. I made a mess of things when I went away, and I wish we didn't lose so many years but marrying you is the greatest gift of my life. Earning your love is my most worthwhile achievement. Starting a family with you is a blessing I don't deserve. But I'm going to live each day trying to be worthy of it."

Tears fill Vivi's eyes, but her smile doesn't falter. It grows.

"I love you with my whole heart and I want to build the most beautiful future with you by my side." I lean forward to kiss her.

Mac blows his nose and Henry clasps his shoulder in support.

"Dec, I've always accepted that God works in mysterious ways. But you being brought back into my life isn't a mystery. I pleaded with Saint Genevieve, for years to light your way. The truth is, I needed the candle. I always made my own path; I just wish I had more faith in knowing that you would be my destination. You've given me the confidence to accept love, to trust, to find my way home to you. Your support is a gift I'll never take for granted. Your love, always so selflessly given, healed the parts of me I thought were lost forever." She places our joined hands on her still flat belly. "And now, we can begin the greatest adventure of our lives. Our little one will be the best parts of both of us, made with so much love. I love you too, Declan Yaeger, and I can't wait to see what's next for us."

Henry and Mac are both openly crying now, and I'd be lying if I said I wasn't bowled over by Vivi's words and the powerful emotions they make me feel.

Vivi and I close the space between us, my hands cupping her cheeks, her fingers finding my sides. Our kiss is sweet and overflowing with promise.

"You guys are so beautiful," Mac weeps.

"I'm happy for you," Henry says.

They wrap us up in hugs and we stand like that for a long moment, a huddle of friendship, love, past, and future, all beneath the willow tree.

"YOU'RE BACK," Mrs. Cleary beams as we step through the door of her bed-and-breakfast.

While Henry and Mac offered to host us, I need to get my wife alone tonight. Since her cousin Alfred is staying at her granddaddy's place, Mrs. Cleary's won out. And, in a way, it's full circle for us.

"We're back," Vivi says, opening her arms for Mrs. Cleary's hug.

"I have the perfect room for you," Mrs. C says. She checks us in and leads us up the stairs to a corner room that overlooks her gardens. An ivory quilt covers the four-poster bed and lacy pillows adorn the headboard. It's much more feminine than the last room I stayed in. Vivi's face lights up as she takes in the floral wallpaper. It's almost like we stepped back in time, to our childhood.

"It's perfect," I tell Mrs. C. "Thank you."

She shakes her head, a smile playing over her mouth. "No, thank you. You've given me much to hope for, seeing the two of you in love again."

Once she leaves, Vivi and I smile at each other. Her expression is soft, tender. She sits on the edge of the bed, and I step toward her, hovering over her frame until she settles back.

"Mrs. Yaeger," I murmur, kissing her mouth.

"I've been Mrs. Yaeger for a while."

"I still like saying it." I lay down beside her, rolling my face toward hers. "I got something for you."

"What's that?"

I pull the ring out of my pocket and take her right hand, slipping it on her middle finger. When she sees it, she darts upright. "This is…this is your mother's ring."

I nod, watching the emotions flicker over her face. Surprise, awe, happiness. God, she's mesmerizing. I could just stare at her all day.

"Want you to have it. If you like…"

She gives me a look. "I love it, Dec. It's, wow, it's beautiful."

The ring is emerald green, the same shade as the rolling hills Da grew up on. A trinity knot adorns both sides, speaking to a rich culture and history.

"Da gave it to my mum when he proposed."

"I remember," she whispers, recalling the story Da told us when we were still kids, having just tasted our first kiss.

"I didn't know he gave it to you," Vivi murmurs.

"I called and asked him for it," I admit.

"And he doesn't mind my wearing it?" She looks up sharply.

"Mind? He's thrilled. Says Mum would be so proud to have a daughter-in-law like you."

This time, Vivi's tears spill over, and I touch her face gently, stopping their trek.

"It came with a promise though," I say.

"What's that?" Vivi holds her hand out, admiring the beautiful stone.

"We're heading to Ireland. Aunt Abilene and my cousins are desperate to meet ya and Da misses you something fierce." I pull the tickets from my pocket and place them on her knee.

She clutches them and checks the date. Surprised, wondrous, glittering eyes meet mine. "We're flying to Dublin on Saturday?"

"We are. For two weeks. I need to be back in time for training camps."

"You'll win the Cup next year." She places her hand over mine.

Losing in the second round of play-offs was tough, but given everything going on in my life at the time, it wasn't as devastating as I thought it would be. Besides... "We're definitely going to win next season. And now, I can take you on a proper honeymoon. I loved Martha's Vineyard, but baby, I need more time with you to celebrate."

She tips her head back and laughs. "Dec, we're already knocked up."

"Doesn't mean we can't practice for the future." I shift closer, placing a hand beside her hip.

She lays back down and I cover her frame, bringing my mouth to within an inch of her lips.

"I want to make lots of babies with you, Vivi."

She tilts her chin up, her lips brushing over mine. "And live in a white house on top of a hill?" she murmurs. An old memory, so faded it's like a dream, ripples through my mind.

Of the plans we made. The promises for the future we dreamed up.

"Fill it up with laughter."

She kisses me hard. "I love you, Declan."

"Me more, sweet Vivi." Then, I show her how much.

In fact, I don't ever stop.

EPILOGUE

TEN YEARS LATER

Vivi

"Mama! Mary put paint in my hair," Leah shrieks, running toward me with a dripping paintbrush.

"Oh dear," I murmur, removing the paintbrush from her hand and pulling her up into my arms. She rests on top of my baby bump. "Your hair still looks pretty, Lee," I tell her. Glancing at Mary, I add, "Paint goes on the door, not on each other."

"I know. I know," Mary mutters.

I set Leah down and redirect my daughters to their task, painting the back door of my old childhood home.

For the past ten years, we lived a full life in Boston. I opened three women's shelters across the city, launched numerous programs centered on female empowerment, and thrived on the connections I created.

Declan and the Boston Hawks won the Stanley Cup last year and after one too many concussions, it seemed like the right season for Dec to hang up his skates. While Alfred and I always shared Granddaddy's home, my cousin married and moved to the Pacific Northwest six years ago and signed over his half of the house to me, around the same time that Liam was born. It was an incredibly generous gift but falling in love and starting a family had softened Alfred's outlook.

So, Declan and I relocated back to Tennessee, back to our sleepy town, to the home where it all began.

"How are you feeling, Ma?" my eldest, Beau, asks.

"I'm fine, baby. Can you help your sisters?" I wince as Leah drags her paintbrush down Mary's arm. Mary shrieks and shoves her sister.

"Paint belongs on the door," Beau tells them, pointing to their half-completed task.

He's nine years old now and has been the greatest help to Declan and me as we welcomed four more babies into the world. Now, I'm twenty-eight weeks pregnant with our sixth child and while my body is tired, I've never felt more fulfilled.

My outlook is bright, and my days are sunny. My work keeps me focused on doing more, doing better, for women and their families. My own family keeps me grounded and humble. My children fill my mornings with endless hugs and butterfly kisses. And my evenings with tall tales and silly pranks.

"There you are." Dec comes around the house, holding hands with Liam, named after Declan's da, and Rosie. "We took a walk to the creek."

"The rope is still there!" Liam announces, excitedly.

"And Daddy's taking us swimming tomorrow," Rosie informs me, all businesslike.

I grin. Dec and I have painted quite the picture of our childhood through bedtime stories. Now, our children have the chance to swim in the creek, learn to read in the public library just down the road, and spend summer afternoons bike riding, capping it all off with a strawberry ice cream dipped in chocolate sprinkles.

"I'll pack you a lunch," I reply.

Rosie gives me a searching look to make sure I'm serious. When she's satisfied, she nods, drops Dec's hand, and runs over to Beau, calling out for Liam over her shoulder.

Dec smiles, wrapping his arms around my growing belly and dropping his chin to my shoulder. "You happy, my Vivi?"

"Happier than I've ever been." I lay my hands over his.

"Look at them," he says.

I do. I stand on top of the hill, in the sunshine, with the white house before me, and watch as the children of my heart, make it a home again. Their giggles are the best sounds I've ever heard.

Dec tugs my hand and leads me to the big willow tree.

I chuckle. "What are you doing?"

"Sneaking a kiss," he says seriously, glancing over his shoulder to make sure the kids aren't following us.

Then, he kisses me with the same hope, heat, and heart as when I was twelve. With the same love as the day I married him. With the same promise of forever on his lips.

THANK you so much for reading Declan and Vivi's second chance, marriage of convenience romance! I hope you loved it!

IF YOU WANT MORE Boston Hawks, make sure to read The Hustler next. Turn the page for a sneak peek!

THE HUSTLER

PROLOGUE — SOFIA

"It's not you, it's me," Don says, gripping my hand with the pressure of a limp noodle. I don't know why that stands out to me, but it does. It's silly really because he's not looking me in the eye and he just delivered one of the most cliché breakup excuses of all time and still…I'm annoyed that he's not gripping my fingers when he says it. It's as if his hold, or lack thereof, is telling of the kind of non-relationship we now have.

"Don, we're supposed to get married in five months," I remind him, my voice much too calm for the blow he's delivering. My body has locked down, a cold drip of disbelief trickling down my spine. My stomach is looped in weaver's knots, the kind my mom would knit while sitting at my hospital bedside, hours on end. My heart rattles painfully, a sudden stop followed by a dramatic lurch that makes me nauseous.

I take stock of my physical reactions to the news and yet, my mind clearly hasn't caught up. Because when I open my mouth again, the most ridiculous thing pops out. "I have a dress fitting in six weeks."

Don's expression twists, his eyes filled with a pity I'm

familiar with. I haven't seen it in years, having beaten my childhood cancer at the age of twelve, but I'd recognize it anywhere. Seeing it now, on his face, somehow hurts more than his calling off our wedding.

He pities me. Me. The survivor, the believer in magic and miracles, the woman without a day to waste. Me, the woman he was planning to marry until…when? What happened?

His response causes a swell of anger to spout in the pit of my stomach. Am I really going to let another person dictate my future happiness? Erase the dream of a family I was mentally painting in my mind? How dare he?

Ooh, that's good. Anger is something I understand. It's something I know how to channel. It's not something I like leaning into, but in this moment, anger feels safer than numbness. Healthier.

"Don, are you fucking kidding me? I don't understand." My voice rises several octaves, a shake at the end of my words. "What, what happened between yesterday and today? I thought we were planning for a future. A family!"

"A family? Like…kids?" He looks confused, which makes my anger soar into fury.

"Of course, kids! We were planning to get married. Why are you ending us?"

Don shakes his head, dropping my hand completely to wipe it down his face. "Sofia," he sighs, "when we met, well, we rushed into things. We barely know each other."

"We've been engaged for eight months!" I holler. While several of my sorority sisters took longer than that just to *plan* their weddings, this has been my longest romantic relationship to date. After two months, I was ready to marry Don. "Almost a year, Don. I moved to Maui to be with you. I left college, I left my volunteer work, I left my life behind to support your career here, with the understanding that we were starting a life together. A fa-family." I stutter on the last word, feeling my heart snap as I say it. I want to grow a family.

For one blink, Don has the decency to look ashamed. But then he locks his expression down and a detachment I didn't think he was capable of washes over his face. "Family, Sofia? You want to talk about family? When were you going to tell me your father is an ex-con, huh?"

I rear back in shock, as if Don's hand just darted out and slapped me. In a way, his words are a knockout blow because... "How do you know that?"

He tosses a hand dismissively. "My parents hired a PI."

"Your parents? A PI? Why?"

"Well, now that we learned the truth about you, your family, don't you think it was a smart idea?" he rationalizes.

The truth about you. Your family.

My heart squeezes painfully, a lack of oxygen pumping through my body at Don's insinuation. No one knows the truth. No one except me, Mom, Dad, and maybe, maybe, my stepfather Mitch. But certainly not Don.

And what the hell does that say that I never confided the truth in my fiancé? I swallow back some of my spite because that *realization* stings too. Deep down, did I know that Don wasn't the one? Other examples zip through my mind. Don taking calls late at night, that one time he came home smelling like Chanel Chance even though I'm a Viktor&Rolf Flowerbomb loyalist, the way his mother has been dragging her feet on our wedding menu.

Wouldn't a normal fiancée question him on those issues? Wouldn't a loving, committed fiancée be able to tell him the whole truth of her past? All the sordid details and painful memories?

Don sighs again, as if breaking our engagement is taking too much of his precious time. "Look, you know how my family is. We're a pillar of the community here, of the *country.*

I can't—*we* can't afford the type of negative press this type of acquaintance would cause."

"Are you referring to our *marriage* as a mere acquaintance? Who the hell wrote your breakup speech? Your mother?"

Don grips the back of his neck and I roll my eyes.

"Whatever, Don. Fine. You found out my big, bad secret. My father used to be in prison."

"For fraud!" He points at me, as if that proves everything.

"Right," I agree, not expanding on it. "And instead of asking me about it, about anything, you and your family decided that our engagement is finished. Is that it?"

Again, he averts his gaze. He nods. He's a fucking coward. Who lets their parents decide who they marry anyway?

"Okay," I say, standing. "Well, then—"

"They're not firing you or anything. I mean, they're happy to settle, give you a package and a recommendation, but after the Felton-Lawrence wedding okay? They really want you to stay on until after the wedding. Heather Felton requested you personally."

Wow. I'm going to take my shoe off and hit him with it. How did I ever think I could marry Don? Worse, belong to and build a *family* with him?

I squint, as if seeing him for the first time.

Right now, after *this* conversation, I don't see the handsome, charismatic, charming man I fell for. I don't recall the way his eyes glistened when he proposed or how his arms caught me when I leapt into them.

Instead, I see a smarmy, indulgent, spoiled man-child who still looks to his parents to run his life. To make his decisions. To inform him of his choices.

For someone who almost missed out on the ability to make choices, that seems like the ultimate waste. A life poorly, unintentionally lived.

Disgust rolls over my tongue and even though I'm hurt, a part of me is also relieved. I don't examine that too closely either. Instead, I roll back my shoulders and stare directly at my ex-fiancé.

"You're right; maybe we did rush into this."

Surprise causes his eyes to widen but then he narrows them, hurt. Welcome to the club, buddy.

I clear my throat. "But that won't be necessary. Consider this my notice. I will stay on for one more month, until the wedding. But not for you or your parents. I'm staying for Heather and Preston. Because I like them. Because they have something real and meaningful, which we clearly did not. The day after their wedding, I'll be gone and the pristine reputation of the Servinos and Lely Prive Resort will remain untarnished by any *acquaintance* with Sofia Carpenter."

Don huffs out a breath, as if I'm being dramatic. Meh, maybe I am. But I'm hurt. Disappointed. In him and in myself. In us.

"I'd like to be moved into my own villa for the next month."

He gapes.

"And don't contact me unless it's work related. We are officially finished. Done. I wish you the best. Well, not really, but I'm trying to be civil," I snap.

Don's eyes widen.

"I'm going to pack my stuff now. Send me a message when my villa is ready." I move to leave his parents' private suite, one similar to the space they were gifting us as a wedding present. Well, that's never going to materialize.

"Wait." Don jumps up. "That's it? Aren't you going to, I don't know, cry?"

I arch an eyebrow. "Over you? No, Don. I have survived the lowest of the low. You breaking up with me without even knowing the truth has demonstrated that I dodged a freaking bullet. Yes, I am hurt. Yeah, I'm a little pissed. But I'm not broken." I flash him a bitter smirk and swipe up my purse. "Men like you can't break women like me."

I make my way back down to the suite I share with Don at the most beautiful, enchanting, private resort on Maui. Eight months ago, I moved here to support Don's career when his parents named him the General Manager of the resort. They gave me a job on the event planning team. It's a fast-paced world, being in operations, but as someone who regularly volunteers to plan galas and charity events at the hospital, or the prison, I adapted quickly.

And I loved having the chance to experience the true beauty of Hawaii.

I enjoyed the magical sunsets, the ones that painted the sky vibrant hues of fiery orange and gold. I was mesmerized by the rich aquatic life. I lived a dream life and I still have the opportunity to do so for another month. Sans Don.

I enter the suite and beeline to my closet. I pull down a bunch of clothes, haphazardly stuffing them into a suitcase. I drop my shoes on top. I'm packing up my bikinis when the first wave of sadness sweeps through me. It intensifies tenfold when I spot the white garment bag at the back of my closet.

My wedding dress. It's the first one I tried on and the moment the soft chiffon whooshed against the tops of my feet, *I knew*. This was the dress. I bought it on the spot and have had it hanging in my closet since that day, almost eight months ago. Pulling out the garment bag, I unzip it to gaze at the dress that made me feel beautiful. Whole.

I blow out a sigh. Whole for the wrong man. I zip up the bag and fold it neatly on top of my suitcase. I feel like a fool. On some level, I believed Don was the one. I brought him to Mom and Mitch's retirement party before they left for a cruise around the world. I took him to a handful of my stepbrother Jesse's hockey games in San Antonio. And perhaps most painfully, I told my Dad about him. I welcomed him into my life and really believed he'd stay there, forever, as a permanent fixture.

It's laughable really. I grew too trusting. Hasn't my past

taught me anything? Nothing lasts forever. All we get are moments, some last longer than others, and this one just came to a sudden end.

I zip up my suitcase and open my laptop. Pulling up the search engine, I type in the information for a flight to San Antonio the day after the Felton-Lawrence wedding. While I wait for the page to load, I pour myself a shot of vodka and toss it back, letting the burn blaze a path of heat to my stomach. Relief quickly follows when I note a flight for that afternoon.

I book it and pick up my cell phone, relocating to the window. I glance out at the sea, my gaze lingering on the curling waves. The ocean is restorative for me, a place that mirrors my moods. Serene and calm, strong-willed and fierce. It can be either a playground or a tempest but both versions comfort me. It's a kinship I formed a long time ago, when I was a bald little girl seeking treatment at Cedars-Sinai Medical Center in LA. We were there for a handful of months and one day, my dad whisked me away from the beeping monitors and IV lines to Venice Beach. That day, the ocean was playful, spraying us with white foam and receding to leave an expanse of seashell treasures behind. Mom and I collected them while Dad took our photos. That day, I wasn't a sick kid, and my parents weren't separated. We were just a family, and it was perfect. For an entire afternoon, it was perfect.

The following month, my symptoms worsened and Mom and Dad legally divorced but my love for that day, for the ocean, remained. I turn away from the window as pressure blooms in my lower back. I press my palm against it, massaging the skin. Ugh, I'm already having physical manifestations of Don's betrayal.

My phone buzzes and I jump.

Don: Villa 34.

The pressure subsides and I grin. The villa feels like a

small victory. Of course, I don't really need a villa, any small room would do. But Don's dismissal of me, his speaking about my father the way he did when he doesn't know anything, *not a goddamn thing*, hurt. My requesting a villa is some petty form of revenge, but now that it's secured, it sure does taste sweet.

In one month, two of America's most prominent families are melding together with the union of Preston Lawrence and Heather Felton.

The resort has hosted many weddings in the eight months I've worked here but this is by far the biggest, the most lavish, and in some ways, the most sincere. While their families are certainly influential and throwing down serious coin on the wedding of the social season, Preston and Heather have been incredibly warm and genuine since I first met them in March when they came to visit the venue. Heather even sent me a bouquet of flowers last week for my birthday.

They're the only reason why I agreed to stay.

I've learned firsthand how cruel, lonely, and empty the world can be. Mostly through my illness but also through Dad's time in prison. On the other side, ironically, both the hospital and the prison offered glimpses of genuine love, sincerity, and commitment. The type that Preston and Heather embody.

I don't care about how this wedding will provide fantastic publicity for the Servino family. It doesn't matter that the Lawrence and Felton names will pull in other high-profile clients. All that matters is that Heather requested me, and I don't want to disappoint her. While Don's dismissal and his parents' disregard stings, Heather's support eases some of my hurt.

Many months ago, we bonded over my volunteer work at the hospital. She even flew in to one of the events in Michigan and, yes, she donated a hefty sum of money, but more than that, she took time chatting and listening to the patients and survivors present. She's one of the shining examples of good I can cling to during this new transition that makes my future feel uncertain.

A prudent woman in my shoes would pray for guidance. Or clarity.

I gather up the rest of my belongings and stack them by the front door.

I've never been prudent. So I'll bank on cold champagne and an ocean view in Villa 34 instead.

ALSO BY GINA AZZI

Knoxville Coyotes Football:

Faked and Fumbled

Surprised and Sacked

Trapped and Tackled

The Burnt Clovers Trilogy:

Rebellious Rockstar

Resentful Rockstar

Restless Rockstar

Tennessee Thunderbolts:

Hot Shot's Mistake

Brawler's Weakness

Rookie's Regret

Playboy's Reward

Hero's Risk

Bad Boy's Downfall

Lock 'Em Down

Boston Hawks Hockey:

The Sweet Talker

The Risk Taker

The Faker

The Rule Maker

The Defender

The Heart Chaser

The Trailblazer

The Hustler

The Score Keeper

Second Chance Chicago Series:

Broken Lies

Twisted Truths

Saving My Soul

Healing My Heart

The Kane Brothers Series:

Rescuing Broken (Jax's Story)

Recovering Beauty (Carter's Story)

Reclaiming Brave (Denver's Story)

My Christmas Wish

(A Kane Family Christmas

+ *One Last Chance* FREE prequel)

Finding Love in Scotland Series:

My Christmas Wish

(A Kane Family Christmas

+ *One Last Chance* FREE prequel)

One Last Chance (Daisy and Finn)

This Time Around (Aaron and Everly)

One Great Love

The College Pact Series:

The Last First Game (Lila's Story)

Kiss Me Goodnight in Rome (Mia's Story)

All the While (Maura's Story)

Me + You (Emma's Story)

Standalone

Corner of Ocean and Bay